TJ

CELEBRATE LIFE
WITH
DEW DROP and TOY

BY

TWILA JUNE

Molly,
Your life radiates
warmth & beauty. My
life is richer just knowing
you.   Twila June
                June 18th, 2003

Printed in Victoria, Canada

National Library of Canada Cataloguing in Publication Data

Alger, Twila June
       Celebrate life with Dew Drop and Toy / Twila June
Alger.
ISBN 1-4120-0023-8
       I. Title.
PZ7.A3779Ce 2003   j813'.6   C2003-901296-4

TRAFFORD

This book was published *on-demand* in cooperation with Trafford Publishing. On-demand publishing is a unique process and service of making a book available for retail sale to the public taking advantage of on-demand manufacturing and Internet marketing. **On-demand publishing** includes promotions, retail sales, manufacturing, order fulfilment, accounting and collecting royalties on behalf of the author.

Suite 6E, 2333 Government St., Victoria, B.C. V8T 4P4, CANADA
Phone   250-383-6864   Toll-free   1-888-232-4444 (Canada & US)
Fax   250-383-6804   E-mail   sales@trafford.com
Web site   www.trafford.com   TRAFFORD PUBLISHING IS A DIVISION OF TRAFFORD
HOLDINGS LTD.
Trafford Catalogue #03-0386   www.trafford.com/robots/03-0386.html

10   9   8   7   6   5   4   3   2

DEDICATION:

Celebrate Life with Dew Drop and Toy is lovingly

dedicated to the **John and Evelyn Teeter family.**

Without them, this book would not have been

possible. Thank you for all the years of joy.

ACKNOWLEDGMENT:

The front cover was designed and illustrated by a friend, **Greg Kabbaz**. He has a God given talent and he uses it for the glory of God.

A NOTE FROM THE AUTHOR:

The reflection at the end of each chapter is a tribute to the hard-working parents or guardians who love their children. All the love that is given them is seen through the eyes of a child.

CELEBRATE LIFE
WITH
DEW DROP and TOY

The Beginning:

You are about to enter a world seen through the eyes of innocent children. This is a secret place where the hearts and minds of children dwell. Let us open the pages and travel through the mind of a child. The year is 1930. The world was in turmoil. The breakdown of the banks and the loss of personal income sent the world into a great depression.

The children in this book escaped poverty and despair by dwelling in a secret place where only love and joy existed. They lived in the hills of rural western Pennsylvania believing that they were the most fortunate children in the world.

CHAPTER 1

KEEPING SECRETS

Living near a little village known to the children as Nannyglow, Dew Drop and Toy were two little girls who had no idea how hard life had become.

Weighing no more than a stone, they were the happiest girls in the whole village. With a song in their hearts, they sang with the sweetest voices that man had ever heard.

Dew Drop and Toy were sisters and closer than two girls could be. Dew Drop was the oldest and wasn't afraid of anything. Toy, the younger of the two, was fragile, very timid, and was afraid of her own shadow. The girls were a year apart and they shared every joy and sadness that came their way.

They lived on a large farm with many animals to keep them company. The farm had rolling hills and its beauty far exceeds anything that you could imagine.

The girls had three brothers. Claude de Ball was the baby and he was very cute and very spoiled. Mr. Blew-it was the oldest and was the girls' protector. Mr. Clagghorn was only three years older than Dew Drop and was always preaching to the girls on how to behave. Dew Drop didn't like her brother telling her anything. After all, he wasn't that much older than her.

One bright sun shining morning, Dew Drop looked out her bedroom window. "I can't believe how much the sun looks like a huge gold penny. "

"Hurry and get up Toy. We have a beautiful day to go see Mr. Warts. He promised us he would show us how to plant flowers in our new flower box. We will have to ask Mum if we can go. Maybe Honey Bee can go with us."

. "Every time Honey Bee goes with us, we get into trouble," said Toy with her lower lip dropping down to her chin. "I don't like to get into trouble and you know it. Honey Bee makes me feel that I'm in her way."

"What is wrong with you, Toy? Honey Bee is our friend."

"Honey Bee is your friend—not mine!"

"Quit your pouting and get dressed."

Toy hurried to get dressed because she wanted to keep up with Dew Drop. Dew Drop was her best friend and boss. She wouldn't think to do anything that Dew Drop didn't like. They were sisters forever and friends for a lifetime.

Looking into the mirror together, they checked their hair and hurried to get downstairs. Running as fast as they could down the stairs, they ran smack dab into their brother, Mr. Clagghorn.

"Where do you girls think you are going?"

Toy looked into his round brown eyes and hurriedly lowered her head, staring at her shoes.

Dew Drop raised her chin and with a lot of courage said, "We are going to breakfast and then go see Mr. Warts—if it's any of your business! Now please step aside big brother. We have a fun day planned."

"Excuse us, please!" Toy, hanging on to her sister's dress, walked around Mr. Clagghorn. The table was set for everyone. Mum baked homemade bread and a jar of apple butter was sitting in the center of the table. Each one had a glass of fresh milk right from the cow. A huge bowl of fruit with sliced apples, peaches, and huge purple grapes made their breakfast complete.

Having a fruit orchard and grapevines on the farm was a real blessing for this family. Everyone chattered and shared their plans for the day.

Looking at the girls, their Daddy said, "Now what are you girls going to do today?"

Toy just stared at the gruff man. Dew Drop raised her chin and said in a small voice, "We want to see Mr. Warts today."

"You girls cannot go by yourself! I thought I made it perfectly clear to you! What part don't you understand? I am your father and as long as you are under my roof you will do what I say. I am telling you this for your own good."

Dew Drop popped up and said, "We aren't going by ourselves! We are going to ask Honey Bee to go with us."

"HONEY BEE! What makes you think taking Honey Bee with you is going to make everything all right?"

"Well you said we weren't to go alone, and if we take her along with us we wouldn't be disobeying you." Smiling into the face of her frowning father, Dew Drop thought she had won that battle, but she was wrong.

Leaning over the table and looking into the girl's eyes, Daddy Waggs said, "Your brother will take you over there! Do you understand?"

Gulping, the girls in a small voice said, "yes!"

After the breakfast table was cleared and they put everything away, the three of them trotted off to see Mr. Warts.

"We aren't going to stay very long because I have a lot of work to do today. You girls have no idea what it is like to work hard."

Dew Drop looking at her brother said, "We can go by ourselves. We won't tell Daddy Waggs if you don't!"

"I'll take you over and come back for you later," said Mr. Clagghorn.

"Okay! Thank you, Mr. Clagghorn. You can be real nice sometimes. Shaking his head and laughing, he took them over to Mr. Warts' cottage."

"I'll see you girls later, and don't get into any trouble!"

Mr. Warts was an old hermit. He lived in a small cottage next to the woods connecting their farm. He was wise as a fox and lived in a fantasy world most of the time. He was a lonely man after his wife died. The girls brought him a lot of joy.

"Hi, Mr. Warts!"

"Well, girls, what can I do for you today?"

"We brought our flower box with us today."

"Well now, let's plant the flower seeds in your box before your brother comes back and ruins all our fun."

"Put the flower box on the picnic table and you girls can pick out what seeds you want."

The girls were thrilled to see all the different colors. There were pansies, daisies, blue bells, marigolds, poppies and irises. What a great selection!

Toy took the watering can down to the creek. She wanted to get water for the beautiful flowers. Leaning over the bank she dipped the can into the water. PLOP! She fell into the creek.

"HELP! HELP! I CAN'T SWIM!"

Hearing her screams, Dew Drop and Mr. Warts ran as fast as they could.

"I CAN'T SWIM!" Toy's head went under and came back up.

"Mr. Warts hurry! I can't swim either," said Dew Drop. *"Oh, please God. Don't let her drown. I promise I will be good if you just help her."*

Mr. Warts stepped into the creek and fell down. He was old and his feet didn't move as fast as they should. Reaching out his hand, he grabbed for her

hand. "Hang on to me and I'll pull you to safety.
Trust me!"

Toy was never so frightened in her life. She
couldn't catch her breath. Water started to fill up
her lungs. She reached out for Mr. Wart's hand and
he pulled her to safety. He laid her on the bank and
with his hands pushed on her back.

"COME ON, TOY GIRL, BREATHE"! Water
trickled out of the corner of her mouth. She coughed
and breathed in great gulps of air. Dew Drop
lowered her head and thanked Jesus that Toy was
safe.

Mr. Warts grabbed a blanket and wrapped it
around Toy's shoulders. How fragile she looked.
Mr. Warts' heart was beating rapidly. He was so
frightened for the frail little girl. Mr. Warts looked
at Dew Drop and thought she looked a little pale.

"Are you all right, Dew Drop? You look like you
need to sit down."

"I'm fine. Toy is the one we need to worry
about."

Looking at Toy, Dew Drop started to laugh. "You look like a drowned rat!"

"Boy, when Daddy Waggs finds out, we are going to be in big trouble." Toy started to cry.

"Stop that crying, Toy! We have to think of something to tell him."

"Mr. Clagghorn will get into trouble, too", said Toy.

"Oh, he can take care of himself," murmured Dew Drop.

Mr. Warts laughed and said, "You have to always tell the truth."

"That's easy for you to say, Mr. Warts!"

Dew Drop took the clothes off Toy and hung them on a limb to dry. Covered from head to toe with the big blanket, Toy began to sneeze. Mr. Warts came outside with a couple cups of hot chocolate and cookies.

"Here, drink up, girls!"

Dew Drop knew they shouldn't be eating cookies before lunch, but they looked so good.

They hadn't had cookies for a long time. She looked at Mr. Warts and smiled. "Thank you", she said.

"Hurry and get dressed. I think Mr. Clagghorn is coming."

Scurrying around, Dew Drop hurried to put on Toy's dress. "Help me, Toy! I can't do it all by myself." Buttoning up the last button on her dress, Dew Drop breathed a sigh of relief that they had just finished on time.

"Let's go girls. We are going to be late."

"Bye, Mr. Warts. We will see you tomorrow."

"I'll keep your flower box here until I see you again. Tell Sweet Pearl I said hello. I saw her the other day and she is prettier than ever."

"Why does he always call Mum, Sweet Pearl?" said Mr. Clagghorn. "He lives in a fantasy world all the time and you girls live in the same world."

"What's wrong with that?" asked Dew Drop.

"I guess the way things are, a fantasy world isn't so bad", he said.

"What do you mean, the way things are?"

17

"Nothing, Dew Drop. Nothing at all."

Sneezing and coughing, Toy struggled to keep on her feet.

"Are you getting sick again, Toy?"

Toy cried, "I don't feel good!" Picking Toy up into his arms, Mr. Clagghorn carried her home.

Mum took one look at Toy and knew she was sick. "Take Toy upstairs and I'll be there in a few minutes." Everyone sat down at the table to eat lunch and Mum went upstairs to take care of Toy.

Dew Drop looked around and asked, "Where is Daddy Waggs?"

"He went to work for a couple of hours. The men have to take turns working only a couple hours a day. He doesn't make much money but it is better than nothing," said Mr. Blew.

Later, Dew Drop read stories to Toy while she was in bed. Neither one of the girls said anything about Toy's accident to their mother. The girls were very quiet and went about their reading as if nothing had happened.

"We have to keep your accident a secret, Toy. You can't tell anyone. Mum and Daddy Waggs will not let us go see Mr. Warts again."

Toy laid her head on her pillow and closed her eyes. She was too sick to argue with Dew Drop, besides Dew Drop always knew the best thing to do.

Brushing her teeth and putting on her pajamas, Dew Drop was finally ready for bed. She kneeled down beside Toy's bed and said her prayers.

DEAR JESUS, I WANT TO BE GOOD BUT I HAVE A PROBLEM WITH THAT. TOY IS ALWAYS GOOD AND SHE NEEDS YOUR HELP TO MAKE HER FEEL BETTER. PLEASE HELP HER JESUS. HELP ME TO BE GOOD AND FORGIVE ME WHEN I'M NOT. GOD BLESS MUM, DADDY, MR. BLEW-IT, MR. CLAGGHORN, AND CLAUDE DE BALL. AMEN! Oh! AND GOD, BLESS MR. WARTS.

Crawling into her bed, Dew Drop tried to sleep. Every time she closed her eyes, Toy started to cough. Mum came in to check on Toy and gave them both a goodnight kiss. "Good night girls, did you say your prayers?"

"Yes Mum! I said them for both of us."

Laughing, Mum said, "I think Toy can say her own prayers. She isn't running a fever. I don't understand how she caught a cold. She is so frail and timid. I expect you to keep her out of trouble, Dew Drop."

"I will Mum, I promise!"

#

Late at night Dew Drop noticed a shadow in their room. It must be the candy-colored sandman, she thought. He sprinkled star dust, bent down and whispered, *"Go to sleep. Everything will be all right."*

The girls' daddy slipped into their room every night. He had to check on the girls to see if they were all right. He looked down into their angel-like faces and smiled. The girls were so little. He secretly loved the spunk that Dew Drop had. He knew she would watch over Toy. Toy was so innocent and frail. He loved all his children. They were God-given and he knew God would not let him down. Oh, yes! He knew God would help them feed and clothe their children.

Closing the door behind him, John leaned his head against the door. Tears filled his eyes. He knew they would always trust God to help them raise their children. The children must grow up knowing they are special and that God loves them.

CHAPTER 2

DADDY'S LITTLE GIRLS

Days passed by and Toy was feeling better.
Mum allowed the girls to go outside and play. "Be
careful girls and stay out of trouble!" Smiling, the
girls decided they would go down to the barn. One
of the cows had a new calf and the girls were just
dying to see it.

Mr. Blew-it was milking the cows and Mr.
Clagghorn was cleaning out the stalls.

"Girls! What are you doing down here?"

"We just wanted to see the new calf," said Dew
Drop. "You don't have to be so grumpy, Mr. Blew-
it."

"We will be careful. You'll see," said Toy.

Climbing the narrow stall, the girls took a look at
the beauty. Leaning over the stall too far, Toy was
so excited she fell in. Dew Drop couldn't believe
her eyes.

"OH NO! HELP! Toy fell in and almost hit the calf."

Mr. Blew-it rescued the little girl. Her dress was all dirty. Scolding the girls, Mr. Blew-it said, "Get up to the house! You girls are always getting into trouble."

They could hear the boys laughing. Dew Drop stomped off dragging Toy behind her.

"Oh those boys make me so-so mad!"

"I'm sorry, Dew Drop, I didn't do it on purpose."

Dew Drop looked at Toy's face and wiped the tears rolling down her cheeks.

"Don't worry, Toy. We will get even with those boys for laughing at us; you'll see."

Walking back to the house they saw Honey Bee running toward them. "Hi girls! What's up?"

"Hi Honey Bee, we were just looking for something to do," said Dew Drop. Toy wrinkled up her face and looked at Dew Drop.

"Let's go swimming in the pond."

"We can't," said Toy. "I just got over a cold."

"Well we can go and chase the chickens," said Honey Bee.

"We can't because Mum is still mad at us; the last time we chased them, they didn't lay any eggs for three days."

"You know what!" said Honey Bee, her eyes sparkling and huge. "We can paint the summer house down by the creek .When I was walking down there, I saw a paint bucket and some brushes. We could paint some stars on it and maybe a moon." [The summer house is a place Mum makes jellies, jams and apple butter--mm-mm good!]

Looking at each other with mischief in their eyes, all three started toward the summer house. After painting for hours, their backs were hurting from all that work. The girls stood back and looked at their art work.

"It doesn't look very good, Dew Drop!"

"Well it doesn't look exactly the way we planned. What do you think, Honey Bee?"

"I think I'm glad this isn't my summer house."

"Daddy Waggs is going to be so mad. We better try to get this paint off our hands and faces. We have more on us than we have on the building."

The girls poured paint thinner on the painting rags and scrubbed their skin as hard as they could.

"Phew! That stinks! My skin is burning Dew Drop." Looking at Toy, Dew Drop noticed that her face was bright red from the paint thinner.

"Let's clean ourselves off in the creek", said Honey Bee.

"We are going to be in the biggest trouble we have ever been in," cried Toy.

"You girls always worry too much", said Honey Bee.

"That's easy for you to say." Dew Drop was so angry because she let Honey Bee get them into trouble again. "You better go home Honey Bee, before I lose my temper."

"You girls are no fun!" said Honey Bee. "I know when I'm not wanted."

On the way home, Dew Drop was planning in her mind what she was going to say to Daddy Waggs. "Let me do the talking Toy."

"You won't have to worry about that!"

Walking into the kitchen the girls were shocked to see Daddy Waggs eating a sandwich.

Looking at the girls he sniffed and said, "What smells?"

Dew Drop raised her chin and said, "We do!"

"What did you girls do this time?"

Looking into her father's eyes, Dew Drop started to explain. "We painted the summer house with stars and half moons. It is so beautiful and I know you will just think we are the best girls in the whole world."

"YOU WHAT! I have to leave for work now, but we will discuss this when I get back. YOU CAN COUNT ON IT! I want you to stay in your room until I get back home. DO YOU UNDERSTAND ME?" Shaking their heads up and down the girls ran upstairs.

Their father couldn't help but smile. He knew Dew Drop was trying to wrap him around her finger. "Beautiful indeed!" He laughed and thought how many times those kids gave him a reason to laugh. He knew that life without them would be very sad.

Giving Sweet Pearl a kiss, he said, "The girls are confined to their room. Take them some milk and fruit for lunch." Winking at his wife, John walked out the door.

"Oh that Honey Bee makes me so-so- mad."

Toy looked into the dark eyes of her sister and said,"This was just as much our fault. We did wrong and now we have to stay in this room and wait for our punishment."

Hugging her little sister, Dew Drop said, "Don't worry Toy. Everything will be all right."

After eating their lunch, the girls waited and waited for Daddy Waggs to return home. They didn't have to wait too long before they heard his footsteps on the stairs. Watching the doorknob turn slowly, their hearts began beating so fast they thought they would not live to see tomorrow.

Standing in front of Toy who was already crying, Dew Drop lifted her chin and said, "This was all my fault."

"I KNOW! "Why are you always getting Toy into so much trouble?"

"I don't know. I guess it just happens!"

"Your brothers are down at the summer house fixing your art work. Think about that for a while!" You girls will stay in your room until tomorrow morning. DO YOU UNDERSTAND ME?"

"Yes Daddy we understand."

"GOOD!"

The girls sat down on their beds and didn't say anything. They had escaped another punishment. This was a piece of cake.

Staring at her feet, Dew Drop started to laugh. She was laughing so hard that the tears started rolling down her cheeks.

"What's wrong, Dew Drop?"

"Stop laughing, it's not funny! Stop it!"

"Well, little sister, Mr. Blew-it and Mr. Clagghorn had to paint the whole summer house. The sun is hot and I bet they are sweating right now. Don't you get it Toy? We had the last laugh after all." Both the girls broke out into laughter.

Taking off their shirts, both boys were sweating and they were not laughing. "Those girls get away with everything", said Mr. Clagghorn. "We are always cleaning up their messes."

Mr. Blew-it just smiled and said, "I guess that is what big brothers are for."

"Well from now on you can be the big brother, I'm just plain tired."

Walking back to the house the boys looked up at the upstairs window and saw Toy and Dew Drop looking out. "Look at those girls. They're laughing at us!" Shaking his fist at the girls, Mr. Clagghorn knew he would someday get even.

The girls felt happy because they finally had the last laugh on their brothers.

OH THE WINDS DO BLOW

THE WAVES DASH HIGH

DEW DROP AND TOY

THEY SAIL ON HIGH

What a great song Mr. Warts made up for them. Singing made them happy no matter what trouble came their way. "Mr. Blew-it and Mr. Clagghorn looked mad at us Dew Drop."

"I don't care! They will get over it soon enough."

The following morning Daddy Waggs and Mum took the girls to Nannyglow. Daddy was hoping to trade some fruit for some flour at the market.

Honey Bee happened to be at the market. "Hi girls!" Honey Bee had on a beautiful sack dress and matching bonnet.

"Oh Honey Bee we are still very angry at you for getting us in all that trouble."

"Well you look like you have survived."

"No thanks to you. You would think that by now I would know better then listen to you."

"I'm going over to see Mr. Warts tomorrow. If you are no longer angry, then maybe I'll see you there tomorrow." Eating her ice cream cone, Honey Bee smiled and said, "Too bad you girls don't have any money to buy one. The chocolate is the best. Bye, Bye."

"OH…OH…that Honey Bee makes me so-so mad! She knows we can't go over to Mr. Warts. Daddy Waggs will not be so easy on us the next time."

Getting flour and sugar for his fruit and eggs, Daddy Waggs whistled the whole way home. The flour sacks were printed with fall leaves. The girls could just imagine how pretty they would look in their new dresses.

Daddy Waggs knew life would get better and all he had to do was keep his growing family fed, clothed, and happy. He smiled at the thought of keeping his family happy. Frowning, he didn't like the idea that his little girls could wrap him around their little finger. No one ever did that before.

#

Late at night the shadow appeared once again in their room. This time he laid down two peppermint sticks on their night stand. Whispering he said, *"Sleep my little beauties I promise everything will be all right."*

John closed the door behind him and prayed for the health and happiness of his children.

CHAPTER 3

FLOATING ON A CLOUD

The days were happy and bright for the two little girls. They had no idea what daily struggles their parents and grandparents had endured.

Grandpa Daveys worked so hard to keep his business from falling into ruin.

Every night Sweet Pearl prayed with all her children and read God's Holy Word from her old tear-stained Bible. The name that Mr. Warts had given her was perfect. She supported and loved all her children. She certainly was a Pearl of Great Price.

The girls loved to visit Mr. Warts. He would push them on a swing that was attached to an old oak tree. Every push seemed to take them higher and higher.

Honey Bee would fly up over the trees and dream what it would be like to fly like a bird.

Dew Drop would fly almost up to the sky and dream what it would be like to ride in an air balloon. It was bright yellow balloon with purple stripes. How beautiful it would be to fly over the mountains and the hills.

Toy would fly so high she dreamed of floating on a white fluffy cloud. They each had their wishes and dreams. The girls laughed and played bringing a ray of sunshine into the lives of every person they touched.

One fall afternoon the girls were playing with their dog Laddie in the pile of leaves that their brothers had just raked. Toy seemed to have very little energy. She had caught another cold and her chest felt heavy.

"I don't feel very good, Dew Drop. Maybe Mum can give me something to help me feel better.

"You never feel very good. "Why are you always sick?" asked Dew Drop. "Mum will probably make me stay inside with you. I want to play a little while longer. I have been in school all

34

day and I need more exercise."

"That's okay Dew Drop. I can go in by myself."

Slowly Toy walked toward the house. Her head hurt and her legs felt heavy. Mr. Blew-it saw her and watched her sway as she walked. He picked her up into his arms and carried her in the house.

"Mum hurry! Toy is real sick."

Hurrying to the kitchen her mother reached out to touch her forehead. She was burning up with fever. "Take her upstairs. Run and tell John we need the doctor."

The whole family was worried. Toy always had a sore throat or an earache, but this time she was really sick. The doctor arrived and Dew Drop was sure he could make her better, after all that's what he was there for.

The doctor closed the door to Toy's room and came into the kitchen. The look on his worried face made Dew Drops' heart sink to her toes.

"I'm sorry John, but Toy is going to have to go to the hospital. She has pneumonia and her fever is very high. Her lungs are filled with fluid and must be drained."

The doctor looked at the worried faces of the parents and knew they were wondering how they were going to pay for her care. Smiling at John he said, "I know money is real tight and in most cases there just isn't any. I will see that the hospital will work something out with you. My main concern is for Toy. Her condition is very serious. I will go with you and see that Toy gets the care she needs."

"Boys! Run down to Aunt Free-da's house and tell her we need her to help out with your baby brother. You boys do the chores and take care of Dew Drop. Free-da will cook and take care of things around here. I don't know when we will be back," said Daddy Waggs.

Aunt Free-da arrived and the kids were glad to see her. Claude de Ball was crying for his food. Mum had goat's milk ready to feed him along with some applesauce. Aunt Free-da was very happy to be able to help with the children.

After the third day Mum came home and was so
tired she couldn't even eat. Tears filled her eyes
when the children asked how Toy was feeling. She
just shook her head and sobbed. She had been at
Toy's bedside and didn't want to leave. Mum had
just come home to get some rest and check on the
baby. Aunt Free-da had him so spoiled that Mum
knew she didn't have to worry.

Daddy Waggs looked at the faces of his children
and just said, "Pray that she gets stronger. Only God
knows if she will get better."

Dew Drop was frantic with fear. This was all her
fault, she thought. She ran up the stairs and fell on
her bed sobbing until she had no strength left to cry.
Mum came into her room and with all the love in
her heart told Dew Drop that this was not her fault.
Hugging her and kissing her forehead, Mum just
held her in her arms.

Mum went to her room to rest and Aunt Free-da
fixed supper. No one was very hungry. Two more
days passed and Toy wasn't any better.

Dew Drop knelt beside her bed and begged God to make Toy well again. *"PLEASE GOD I KNOW YOU HAVE THE POWER TO HEAL MY SISTER. I MISS HER VERY MUCH. SHE IS PART OF MY HEART. I FEEL EMPTY WITHOUT HER. IF I COULD JUST SEE HER AND TALK TO HER MYSELF, I KNOW SHE WOULD GET WELL FOR ME. SHE LOVES ME A LOT, YOU KNOW. I PROMISED YOU BEFORE THAT I WOULD BE GOOD AND FAILED. PLEASE GIVE US ANOTHER CHANCE. HELP DADDY AND MUM, TOO. THEY ARE SO WORRIED AND TIRED. EVEN MY BROTHERS HAVE BEEN GOOD. THERE IS NO JOY IN OUR FAMILY ANYMORE. I LOVE YOU! PLEASE HELP US; WE NEED YOU NOW MORE THAN EVER.*
AMEN."

Dew Drop crawled into her bed and turned out the light. The moon was shining bright and it looked like a big ball of fire. The shadow filling her room made Dew Drop shiver with fear. The branches from the big oak tree filled her room with scary shadows and made her heart skip with fright.

Closing her eyes she could see herself sitting on the big swing. Mr. Warts was swinging her higher and higher. She was laughing and the higher she swung the louder was her laugh. She kept telling Mr. Warts to swing her higher and higher.

She swung so high clear up to the sky.

Dew Drop and Toy they sail on high.

Dew Drop was flying high in the sky, but she couldn't find Toy. "Toy, where are you? I can't find you!"

"Here I am, Dew Drop."

"Where?"

"Right beneath you on a cloud."

Looking under her swing, Dew Drop saw Toy lying on a beautiful white cloud.

"Look Dew Drop! Here comes a cloud for you! Just let go of your swing and let yourself fall."

"I can't; I'm afraid!" Dew Drop hung on so tight to the swing that her hands were bright red.

"You are never afraid. Come on its fun, just let yourself fall."

Dew Drop closed her eyes real tight and let go of the swing. It's only a dream she thought, it can't hurt too much! Falling, and her heart pounding at a rapid pace, she had never felt so free or so alive. PLOP! She fell right into the center of a beautiful cloud. The cloud was warm and soft.

Drifting toward Toy, she saw her sister's beautiful face. She didn't look sick. "What are you doing here Toy?"

"I'm reaching for the hand of God," she said. "I can feel Him close by, but I can't see Him."

"NO! NO! TOY! Reach for my hand instead. I need you. Please don't leave me."

"You worry too much, Dew Drop. Just keep floating on this beautiful cloud. It is so peaceful up here and God is close by to keep us safe."

Toy's right leg was hanging over the cloud and she was just swinging it back and forth. She didn't seem to be afraid at all.

"It's time for you to go back, Dew Drop. The swing is flying high for you to grab on to it. Hurry! You don't want to miss your ride back to the farm. Give everyone a big kiss for me and tell them I am reaching for the hand of God. Don't cry Dew Drop, please don't cry!"

"NO! NO!" cried Dew Drop.

"The swing is coming Dew Drop. Hang on real tight." She could hear Toy sing:

> DEW DROP AND TOY
>
> HEARTS FILLED WITH JOY
>
> THEY SING SO HIGH
>
> CLEAR UP TO THE SKY
>
> And they sing
>
> In the sweet bye and bye

Toy's voice was fading and so low that Dew Drop couldn't hear it anymore. Broken- hearted Dew Drop let go of the swing and started falling to the ground. Screaming and crying, her heart pounded wildly as she fell. Through the fog, she heard Mr. Blew-it speaking softly to her.

41

"Wake up, Dew Drop. You had a bad dream."

Dew Drop opened her eyes and let the tears roll down her face. "What time is it?"

"It's around four o'clock. You won't have to get up for a long time. It's Saturday and you can sleep in. Are you all right Dew Drop?"

"I don't know! I feel like I lost something precious but I don't know what it is."

"Go back to sleep! Daddy didn't come home last night but I have a feeling when he comes home, he will have some good news to tell us."

"Oh I hope you are right," said Dew Drop.

Tears spilling on her pillow and with a terrible ache in her heart, Dew Drop pulled the covers up around her head. She tried to remember her dream but she couldn't bring it back.

The next morning everyone was eating breakfast when Mum and Daddy came in the door. Every eye was on the face of their father. Their hearts beating faster and faster they were sure it was about to explode.

Aunt Free-da was the first to speak, "How is the little lamb?"

Mum sat down and started to cry. "Toy was so sick. Her temperature rose higher and higher. They told us that she couldn't live through the night. We just held her and prayed. We were trying to prepare ourselves for the worst. She started to come out of her coma just before four o'clock this morning. Toy mumbled something about a cloud and talking to Dew Drop. She didn't make much sense, but we were so excited she could talk we didn't care what she said."

Dew Drop was stunned. She heard the words that Toy had said, and her dream started coming back to her. The clouds…listening to Toy sing. She was reaching out for God's hand for healing, and Dew Drop thought she was reaching for His hand to go to heaven.

Dew Drop knew no one would believe her if she told them her dream. She was going to keep all these things close to her heart. Raising her eyes to heaven she whispered, *"Thank you, God, for all the miracles you have given us. Sometimes you give us blessings and we miss them. I always look to you when I am in trouble. Help me to look for you even when things are good."*

God's word tells us…You will seek me and find me, when you seek for me with all your heart.

JEREMIAH 29:13 (NIV)

CHAPTER 4

A WRINKLED FACE

One month after Toy got sick; she was able to come home from the hospital. Daddy Waggs was carrying her in his arms. She looked so pale and beautiful. She had on a pretty dress and white leggings. Looking at Toy's feet, Dew Drop couldn't believe her eyes. She had on a pair of black patent leather shoes. Those were the shoes that Dew Drop had wanted for a very long time.

It just wasn't fair! Green-eyed jealousy took over Dew Drop's heart. She had waited for weeks for Toy to come home and now she couldn't see anything but her own jealousy.

Grabbing her coat she ran out of the house toward the barn. What is wrong with me? Sobbing with rage, Dew Drop fell into a huge stack of straw. She knew her feelings were wrong but she just couldn't help herself.

Everyone was thinking of Toy, and no one even cared that Dew Drop was heart broken. Day after day Dew Drop was pushed farther and farther into the background. When the final day arrives for Toy to come home, she is wearing the pair of shoes that Dew Drop wanted for herself.

Trying to reason with herself, Dew Drop couldn't believe her Mum had bought Toy those shoes. Crying and sobbing, Dew Drop felt that no one loved her.

She had no idea how long she laid in the straw when she heard a noise sounding like footsteps. It's probably her brother, Mr. Clagghorn, coming to find her. She turned her head around and saw a shadow against the horse stall. "Who's there?"

No one answered. Picking up a pitch fork to protect herself, Dew Drop yelled again. "Who's there?"

"Don't get into such a huff…it's only me!"

"Who are you? I have never seen you before and I'm not sure I even like you."

Looking into the face of a young girl, Dew Drop said, "I don't know you. I have never seen you before."

"Oh yes you have; plenty of times!"

The girl looked into Dew Drop's dark eyes and said, "Don't I look familiar?"

Dew Drop thought she looked like someone she knew but couldn't quite place her. She was actually pretty homely, thought Dew Drop.

"Why does your face look so wrinkled?"

The girl raised her chin and said to Dew Drop, "Maybe you could answer that for yourself."

"How could I answer that? Today is the first day I ever saw you."

"Look in my eyes, Dew Drop!"

"How do you know my name?"

"Just look into my eyes!"

Dew Drop walked closer to the girl and looked into dark eyes very much like her own. Startled, Dew Drop stepped back. "Those are my eyes! How could you have my eyes?"

"I think you better sit down! I know your name and have your eyes because I AM YOU!!"

"NO! NO!" "I hate to burst your bubble but I have a pretty face and your face is all wrinkly."

"See how you look when you are jealous and feeling sorry for yourself? I am your inner self…known as your conscience. Right now I look pretty ugly."

Dew Drop tried to reason with herself. "I don't believe you. You are just trying to scare me."

"Are you scared, Dew Drop?"

"You want me to be scared, don't you? I don't like you and I want you to go away. Leave me alone!"

The little girl looking at Dew Drop said, "I can't leave you alone. You are very angry and you need to see yourself for who you are."

Lowering her head, Dew Drop felt very ashamed of herself. Speaking very softly, Dew Drop said, "it was those shoes that made me so angry. I guess I was more hurt than angry. Toy was wearing those black patent leather shoes that I wanted so bad. Mum told me we couldn't afford those shoes."

"Oh I see! Your sister was sick and almost died. You are so angry because she wore a new pair of shoes home from the hospital."

"Those were the shoes I wanted," said Dew Drop.

"Do you think she wore them home to make you jealous?"

"Of course not! She didn't even know I wanted them."

"Oh I see! It's your mother's fault!"

"Well I couldn't believe that she bought them for Toy when she knew how bad I wanted them."

"Oh I see!"

"Quit saying that! What do you see?"

"I see how selfish you are. Why don't you ask your mother why she bought shoes for a little girl who was dying? Maybe she needed a lighter pair of shoes on her little feet. It makes me wonder how much you really love your sister."

"Do you remember the words you promised God when you thought Toy would die? Let me refresh your memory:"

'PLEASE GOD I KNOW YOU HAVE THE POWER TO MAKE TOY WELL. I MISS HER SO MUCH. SHE IS PART OF MY HEART.'

"Shall I go on?"

"NO! NO!" Tears rolling down Dew Drop's face she said, "will God ever forgive me?"

"Of course He will forgive you, if you ask him to."

Kneeling down on the barn floor, Dew Drop let all her angry emotions fade away as she poured her heart out to God.

After she was finished praying, Dew Drop looked around for the little girl. "Where did she go? I wonder if I will ever see her again. Boy, I hope it is a long time before she shows her wrinkled face around here again!"

Feeling lighter, she skipped all the way to the house. Closing the kitchen door behind her, Dew

Drop searched for Toy. She was lying on the couch with her arms around her doll.

Dew Drop looked into the pale face of her sister. She bent her head and started to cry. All her pent-up emotions came pouring out. Toy reached out her hand and touched Dew Drop's hand.

"Don't cry, Dew Drop. I'm feeling a lot better."

Dew Drop raised her head and wiped the tears from her eyes.

"We will be running and playing again real soon. When you are at school, I'll sleep and rest so we can play when you get home."

Tears blurred Dew Drop's eyes. Dew Drop never knew that loving someone could hurt so much.

Days and weeks passed and Toy was finally starting to get her strength back. Mr. Blew-it and Mr. Clagghorn brought some kids over to the farm so they could wave at Toy through her bedroom window. They were happy that Toy was getting better. Mum was glad when Dr. Roads came to check on her progress. He would just shake his head and tell them what a miracle it was that she survived.

Toy had a big scar on her back where they drained her lungs. Every time the family saw it, they were reminded that they almost lost a very precious gift.

#

Late at night the shadow appeared in their room again and again. Dew Drop felt his presence this night, but couldn't open her eyes wide enough to see him.

It must be the candy-colored sandman again, she thought.

He sprinkled his star dust and whispered, *"Go to sleep. Everything will be all right."*

John closed the girls' door behind him. The weight of the whole world was once again on his shoulders. Tears blurred his eyes and he wondered what he was going to do about all the bills that were coming in.

The hospital was going to help him apply for aid from the government so he could get the hospital bills paid. Doc Roads never sent him a bill. John never asked anyone for anything in his whole life. He was sure that he was a failure. Walking slowly to his room and with a heavy heart, John broke down and cried.

CHAPTER 5

THE BLIZZARD

The winter was very cruel and harsh, but how could you describe its great beauty. The hills and the mountains were alive with music of the blustery winds. They sang to you day and night. The creeks and the streams were running slowly with chunks of ice drifting away into the magic night.

A huge moon was shadowed with a bright circle sending moon beams down on a blanket of white snow. The ice was hanging heavy on the trees making them look like beautiful crystal glass. The sun shining bright on the new fallen snow brought twinkles of diamonds to your eyes. All of this beauty makes you wonder what it would be like to see the glory of God.

Dew Drop and Toy loved the beautiful snow. Toy had to stay inside but Dew Drop made angels in the snow to make Toy laugh. Her face would be pressed against the window watching the boys make her a snowman. Her laughter brought joy to the whole family.

Sometimes the heavy snow made it hard for the children to walk to school. They walked at least two miles a day. They wore a heavy coat and a knitted scarf around their face. Dew Drop wore heavy brown leggings on her legs to keep her warm. Mum made them mittens and gloves. The heavy boots they wore made it hard to trudge through the heavy snow.

Dew Drop and Mr. Clagghorn went to the same one-room school. Mr. Blew-it would walk them part way to school then he would take another road to his school.

One blustery cold day the children struggled to get to school. Each step they took, the wind would blow them back two steps.

"Maybe we should go back home", said Mr. Clagghorn. "I'm cold and I know Dew Drop is cold too."

Mr. Blew-it teased them and said, "Go ahead and go home, little babies. This is just a nice brisk winter day. Only babies would give up and go home."

They could hear his laughter ring in their ears. Anger took over their bodies and their feet became lighter. Trudging along in the snow the children were exhausted

They came to the fork in the road and they took their own path to the school. The most beautiful sight was seeing the little school house. Opening the door, the wind blew them inside. The teacher was writing on the blackboard. She turned around and saw the snow-covered children.

The pot-bellied stove was warm and inviting and the teacher smiled and said, "I guess you are the only two here today." The school room was empty. Mrs. Wicks saw the disappointment on their faces.

"I know you struggled to get here and all is not lost. We will play some games and when you are good and warm, you can go home. We will dismiss school for the rest of the week because of Thanksgiving. I have a surprise for you!"

Mrs. Wicks pulled out a huge box of clothing. The children's eyes were huge and sparkling. Inside the box were shirts, dresses, gloves, pretty colored stockings and heavy sweaters.

"Do you think you can get them home?"

The children were so excited. They said, "Oh, yes!"

The sun was shining by the time they left the school. They pulled and yanked at the box. The children were going to get that box home no matter how hard it would be for them.

They stopped at the fork in the road. "Do you think Mr. Blew-it will be going home early, too?"

"No! We better get moving. Look at the sky!"

The sun had faded under the dark clouds, and the clouds were rolling in fast.

"We are going to get into a snow storm. We better hurry! Come on, Dew Drop. We better hurry!"

They were a little more than half way home before the snow started to fall. The wind picked up and the swirling snow became blizzard-like conditions.

They couldn't see in front of them. Dragging the heavy box made it almost impossible to walk.

"We have to leave the box, Dew Drop".

"NO! We need those clothes! I won't leave them."

Mr. Clagghorn was only three years older than Dew Drop, but he knew the peril they were in.

"We can hide the box under that tree and come back for it after the storm."

"NO! Come on, help me drag it."

"Stop it Dew Drop! The temperature is dropping and we have to keep moving."

They knew they couldn't make it home until the snow stopped.

"Let's go to Mr. Rooks' shed. We can stay there until the storm stops. We have to hurry or we might freeze to death."

Dragging the box, they searched for the shed.

"I know it's here somewhere. It has to be here."

They were freezing and time was running out for them. Crying and praying, they finally saw the top of the shed.

"There it is!" shouted Mr. Clagghorn.

Dragging the box with them, they rushed inside the old shed. The box was tearing apart and they had lost some of the clothes. Crying, Dew Drop fell to the floor.

"I'm scared, Mr. Clagghorn."

"We at least have protection from the storm," he said.

"We lost some of the clothes and I really needed them," cried Dew Drop!

"I needed those clothes, too, but we should be thankful for the clothes we have!"

Mr. Clagghorn knew they were in grave danger of freezing. Some how the clothes they lost didn't seem to matter. He pulled out some of the heavy sweaters and socks.

"Here, put these on. At least we can stay warmer." Cuddling closer to each other, they were so tired they fell asleep.

*

Mr. Blew-it was sent home early and he made it home before the storm reached blizzard conditions.

"Where are those children?" Sweet Pearl was becoming panic stricken.

"Maybe the teacher kept them at school, Mum. She probably saw the storm coming and made them stay where it was warm and safe."

Mum looked at her oldest son and said, "I hope you are right." The problem was that neither one of them believed it. They were sure the children were caught in the storm.

Toy was looking out her bedroom window and watching the snow fall. She knew it was past time for Dew Drop and Mr. Clagghorn to be home. Running down the stairs she saw Mum and Mr. Blew-it looking outside.

"Where are they, Mum?"

"I don't know, Toy."

Toy looked at Mr. Blew-it and blurted out, "What are you doing here, Mr. Blew-it? You're supposed to be with them."

Looking at him with accusing eyes, she said, "You are older and you are to protect them."

Mum put her arms around Toy and whispered, "You aren't to blame your brother. This isn't his fault. I think you should tell your brother that you are sorry."

"NO! I WON'T!" She looked into the eyes of her brother and cried, "If anything happens to them, it will be your fault!" Toy ran up the stairs as fast as her little legs could run.

Sweet Pearl said to her son, "She doesn't mean it. She is just worried and doesn't know how to express herself."

"Oh! She expressed herself all right." Mr. Blew-it lowered his head and blamed himself. He couldn't help but remember how he teased them and prodded them on when they wanted to return home.

He made them angry and Mr. Blew-it wished he
would have kept his big mouth shut. Maybe they
would be home safe now.

Hours passed and the sun had gone down. The
blizzard finally stopped, but it was too dark to go
out and look for them. Daddy Waggs had been at
work and waited for the storm to stop before he
came home.

"Boy, what a storm we had!" Looking at his
wife's worried face he said, "what's wrong now?"

Toy had burst out crying and ran into her father's
arms. "Dew Drop and Mr. Clagghorn are out in that
storm."

"What!"

"They were probably sent home early. Mr. Blew-
it came home without them and I am mad at him,"
Toy cried!

"We are not sure they even left the school," said
Daddy Waggs. He tried to calm himself. He knew
in his heart that his children were out in that storm
somewhere.

"The moon is bright and we could go to the school and look for them. Get your coat and some flashlights. The lantern could help us, too. Hurry!"

Turning to his wife, he smiled and said, "don't worry everything will be all right!"

*

"Mr. Clagghorn, wake-up! The storm is over. Wake-Up! The moon is bright and maybe we could walk home."

Mr. Clagghorn woke up with a startled look on his face. "Where are we?"

"We are in Mr. Rooks' shed. Remember?"

"The storm must be over. Boy! Those sweaters are really warm. I almost forgot where we were."

"Daddy Waggs is probably looking for us," said Dew Drop.

"We better stay here where it is warm and start home tomorrow after the sun comes out. We might get hurt if we can't see where we are going, Dew Drop."

"I'm scared and I want to go home."

"Here, pile these clothes on top of you and we can huddle together to save our warmth. Dew Drop looked at her brother and said, "Are you scared?"

"No! Of course I'm not scared. Let's pray and go to sleep. We will go home tomorrow."

NOW I LAY ME DOWN TO SLEEP, I PRAY THE LORD MY SOUL TO KEEP. IF I SHOULD DIE BEFORE I WAKE, I PRAY THE LORD MY SOUL TO TAKE.   AMEN.

"Now go to sleep. I believe you covered all the bases with God just in case something happens during the night!"

Dew Drop looked at her brother and said, "You're making fun of me, aren't you?"

"NO! I just haven't heard you pray that child's prayer in a long time. You are closer to God than that. Just tell Him you are afraid and you need Him to keep you safe."

Dew Drop said a silent prayer and tried to close her eyes. She could hear the wind blowing and she heard a coyote howling at the moon. Fear gripped her heart and she snuggled closer to her brother. *"Please God help Daddy Waggs find us,"* Dew Drop whispered in the wind.

Daddy Waggs and Mr. Blew-it drove to the school house. The children weren't there!

Fear caused their hearts to beat faster. What were they going to do? They had gotten stuck in the snow drifts three times. They drove the big heavy tractor and still couldn't keep from getting stuck. They had to find the children soon or they would be in serious trouble. Driving slowly back towards home they noticed some clothes lying along the side of the road.

"What are those clothes doing here? Get me the lantern!"

Stopping the tractor they followed the string of clothing.

"Look Daddy! "Isn't that Mr. Rooks' shed?"

Running as fast as they could, they pushed the door open to the shed. There they were, holding clubs in their hands. The children were ready to defend themselves.

"Oh, Daddy Waggs," cried Dew Drop, running non-stop into her father's arms. "I knew you would find us."

"Come on children. Let's go home!"

Daddy Waggs hugged his children and asked them if they were all right. Dew Drop and Mr. Clagghorn looked into the eyes of their beloved father. Fear left them and peace filled their hearts.

"We are just fine now," they said.

All the way home the children told Mr. Blew-it about the clothes that Mrs. Wicks gave them. "We lost some of them, but we can look for them tomorrow," said Mr. Clagghorn.

"You won't have to look for them," said Mr. Blew-it.

"Why?"

"We found them and picked them up while we were looking for you. The clothes led us right to the shed."

The children were so glad that the clothes were

found. They all headed home. This would be a day they wouldn't soon forget.

Mum had supper ready and greeted the children with tears in her eyes. Daddy Waggs looked at his children and said, "When the weather is bad, all of you will stay home from school!" All eyes were glued to their Daddy.

"I hope I have made myself perfectly clear! DO YOU UNDERSTAND?" The children shook their heads up and down and looked at the man they loved with all their hearts.

#

Late that night a shadow appeared in the girls' bedroom again. Dew Drop and Toy couldn't wake up enough to see who it was. In their mind they thought it must be the candy-colored sandman again. He tiptoes in their room every night, sprinkling star-dust and whispering, *"Go to sleep. Everything will be all right."*

John closed the door behind him. He had just
seen the boys and needed to see his girls. He had
never been as scared as he was tonight. He was
supposed to be tough, and the children had a way of
making a tough man fall to his knees.

Every father has fears for his children. God is
their protector. No matter how hard he tries, he
knows in his heart that God is the answer to all his
problems.

Thank you God, again and again for protecting
and loving my family.

CHAPTER 6

MAGIC STARS

Two weeks before Christmas, Mr. Winter blew its fury with huge snow drifts measuring seven to eight feet. Trying to feed the animals caused serious problems. The big kerosene tractor with big iron wheels and a wide plow was the only way to open a road to the barn.

Christmas was moving in fast and everyone was busy making their Christmas presents. The girls could hardly wait until the tree was cut and brought home. They were busy making the decorations for the tree. They made garland with colored paper and threaded popcorn to make the tree more beautiful.

Mr. Clagghorn and Mr. Blew-it had gone with their Daddy to bring home the tree. This was an exciting time for the whole family. The girls were so excited they pressed their faces against the window until they were out of sight.

"What's taking them so long, Dew Drop? They have been gone a long time."

"It hasn't been very long, Toy. You are just anxious."

The boys couldn't decide which tree was the best one.

"Come on, boys. We don't have all day."

"Let's cut down this tree. It is fuller and straighter than the others," said Mr. Blew-it.

John took the big saw and started to cut down the tree. 'TIMBER!" he shouted! What a beautiful tree they thought.

Dragging the tree, they hooked it to the back of the sleigh. The horses struggled through the snow to drag the tree and pull the sleigh.

"Finally, there here!" shouted Toy.

"Stay out of the way so you don't get hurt", said Mum.

The boys cut off the bottom of its branches and started to bring the big tree into the house. The girls watched the boy's struggle with the tree. The tree

was set in the corner and turned around. The girls'
eyes were as bright as diamonds.

"What do you think, girls?"

"It looks so beautiful!"

Daddy Waggs walked in from the barn and
looked at their prize. "We did good, boys. Yes, sir!
We did real good!"

The rest of the day they decorated the tree. Mum
had crocheted some snowflakes and made a
beautiful star for the tree. The multicolored lights
were plugged in and tinsel was placed on the tree.
No one could have a more beautiful tree, not even
Honey Bee.

Christmas was special because it was the
birthday of Jesus. The family made a birthday cake
and a birthday party was planned. Gifts were placed
under the tree and a special card was made for the
Baby Jesus. This time of year was magical and the
girls had dreams that they only told God about.

One night the girls were looking out their
bedroom window. The stars were shining and

dancing in the sky. The night was clear and a huge full moon brightened the dark night.

"Look at that bright moon," said Toy. "The sky seems to be expressing its Joy of the Christmas season."

"What does the sky know about Christmas?" asked Toy.

"I don't know for sure, but I only imagine they celebrate Christmas too."

When the girls laid in their beds that night, Dew Drop was thinking about the sky. The stars were dancing in a circle and the moon had a bright smile on its face.

Drifting off to dreamland, Dew Drop felt like she didn't weigh anything and floated off into the sky. Smiling and looking at the stars and planets, Dew Drop was in awe of their beauty. She knew that no one would ever believe the beauty of the heavenly skies. While she was busy looking around, she heard a small voice calling to her.

"Who and what are you?" said a bright star.

"My name is Dew Drop and I am a little girl.
"What is your name?"

"My name is JOY!"

Dew Drop looked at the star and wondered why
the stars had names.

"I am made to bring a shining light into a dull
world. God named me and I am special. My job is
to bring joy into the lives of unhappy creatures.
They look at me, and just my very presence brings
them joy. This is my special gift to the world."

The star looked at Dew Drop and asked her what
her special gift was to the world.

Thinking, Dew Drop said, "My special gift was
to tell children the good news that God loves them."

"How many children did you tell that good news
to?"

Taken by surprise Dew Drop hung her head and
said, "Not many."

"WHAT!! Then I guess you haven't done a very
good job with your special gift."

Just as Dew Drop opened her mouth to defend

73

herself, another star danced toward her.

"Hi! My name is SWEET SPIRIT. We have a lot
of friends in this heavenly realm. My best friend is
MERRY HEART! She helps me to remain a sweet
spirit."

"Turn around and you can see MR. BEAMERS,"
said the sweet little voice. "Everyone thinks he is
the man in the moon but there is no such person.
MR. BEAMERS is the man behind the moon. Look
at his face and you can see his eyes and nose
through the moon's bright face."

Dew Drop looked puzzled.

"What's wrong little creature?"

"I'm not a creature! I'm a little girl! My name is
Dew Drop and you hurt my feelings."

"OH! I feel sorry for you. I thought you were as
special as we are."

Anger swept through Dew Drop. "I am special
and I'm more important to God than you are."

The little star looked at Dew Drop's face and
said, "I didn't mean to hurt your feelings. You

better move on because you are angry. Anger has no place in our heavenly realm. If we become angry, then our beauty is destroyed. What about your world, Dew Drop? Does your beauty get ruined when you get angry?"

Right away Dew Drop thought of the little girl with the wrinkled face. How ugly her face had become when she was jealous and angry. "Please forgive me. You are very beautiful and I had no right getting angry with you," said Dew Drop.

The beautiful star smiled and told her she could come and visit anytime she left her anger at home. Looking at the sky with all its beauty, Dew Drop started to drift back into her own world.

The next morning the sun was shining very bright on the cold ground. Dew Drop tried to remember what her dream was about the night before, but as always, she forgot.

Today was the day before Christmas and all through the house was the excitement of this very special favorite holiday. There wasn't much money to buy gifts, but that didn't seem to bother this little family.

The girls made cookies and played with Claude de Ball. He was only a baby, but he knew that something special was going to take place this night.

Everyone sat around the tree singing Christmas carols and the time came to light the birthday cake. They all sang happy birthday to the baby Jesus. The special bond of love was wrapped around them.

When twilight came, the magic of the Christmas Eve was filling the family with joy and peace. The stars looked brighter than usual. They no longer held a great mystery to Dew Drop, but she didn't know why.

Toy and Dew Drop thought the stars were winking and waving at them, and who knows, maybe they were.

Late that night when Dew Drop and Toy drifted off to sleep, three little stars came close to their bedroom window. They whispered, "MERRY

BRIGHT CHRISTMAS, and may God give you JOY, a SWEET SPIRIT, and a MERRY HEART for all the rest of your days and nights.

Peace entered the hearts of the two sleeping children. Peace that only God can give.

CHAPTER 7

THE TRUSTING FOX

Spring arrived late and with it came floods from the winter thaw. The tulips and the crocuses were trying to peak their heads out of the box that belonged to the girls.

Mr. Warts was glad that the long hard winter was finally over. He thought about the girls he loved as his very own. He even missed Honey Bee. Mr. Warts would smile when he thought of the girls.

He hadn't felt well this winter. His old heart was beating faster and his old legs would hardly move at all. He was hoping that he could enjoy one more summer with the girls. He knew that since winter was over the girls would come and visit him soon.

"Hello, Mr. Warts! Are you here?"

"Of course I'm here! I was just thinking about you girls."

"It's Saturday and Mr. Clagghorn walked us over to your cottage. We can't stay long because Daddy Waggs doesn't know we are here. We just wanted to make sure you survived the long, hard winter."

"How nice of you girls to think about me. I am fine as frog hair and twice as nice."

Laughing, the girls were happy to hear his own familiar way of talking.

He was so alone and no one saw him this past winter. Mr. Warts looked at the girls and he knew they had really grown since the last time he saw them.

"Toy girl! I heard you had been real sick awhile back," said Mr. Warts.

"That was a long time ago, Mr. Warts." Standing to her full height, Toy stuck out her little stomach and patted it with her hands.

"See I am getting big," she said.

"Of course I can see how big you are," laughed Mr. Warts.

"Girls! I have a big surprise for you. Let's take a walk over to the old shed by the creek."

The girls put on their coats and hurried to keep up with Mr. Warts.

"What's the surprise?" said Toy.

"You will have to wait and see."

Walking along with Mr. Warts, Dew Drop noticed how slow he was walking.

"Are you all right, Mr. Warts?"

"I guess, I'm not a spring chicken anymore."

Toy looked at her sister and with a smile said, "I have never seen a chicken like that."

Laughing, Mr. Warts patted Toy on her head and said, "Yes sir! I really missed you girls!"

Reaching the shed, they all looked inside. The sun was bursting through a small window and lying in the corner was a beautiful fox and her babies.

"I found her down by the spring. She was caught in a man-made trap and was desperate. The scared animal had babies close by and would have died trying to protect them."

The girls were awestruck at the sight of the mother and her babies.

Mr. Warts said, "She knew I wouldn't hurt her and I just wanted to help her. Animals have a built-in radar system to know who they can trust and who they can't trust. I fixed her leg and brought her and her babies here so she could heal."

"Well, girls! What do you think?"

Dew Drop couldn't keep her eyes off the fox. She had never seen a wild animal this close. She blinked her eyes and stared at the beauty.

"Oh, Mr. Warts, I haven't seen anything so beautiful in my whole life."

Toy was afraid to look into the eyes of such a wild creature. Hiding behind Mr. Warts, Toy said, "What have you named her?"

"She isn't a pet. We must let her go as soon as her foot is healed. Wild animals are meant to live in the wide open spaces." Scratching his head, Mr. Warts said, "I suppose I will have to let them go in another week."

81

Dew Drop was trying to figure out how many days they had left to visit the fox. "Let's see. We have five school days and Saturday. We aren't allowed to visit on Sunday because we have to go to church. We go to church twice on Sunday."

"Do you go to church, Mr. Warts?"

"No! I haven't gone to church for a long time, and I don't expect to."

"Why?"

"My Ruthie liked church better than I did and after she died, I quit going."

Dew Drop touched Mr. Warts' arm and said, "You can go with us if you want to."

Mr. Warts looked at Dew Drop and hung his head. "No! I think I'll pass this time."

"Okay, but you are always welcome to go with us," said Dew Drop.

Walking back to the cottage, the girls begged Mr. Warts to swing them on the swing. Toy wanted to be first and she squealed with laughter when he swung her higher and higher.

Toy was pretending to be back on a fluffy white cloud, but this time she was afraid. *Where is God?* She felt a small flutter in her heart and then she knew. God was there right beside her all the time. She couldn't see Him but she knew He was there. He was always right there protecting her and loving her as He said He would.

"Hurry Toy! It's my turn."

Toy finally came back to the ground and with a secret smile held the swing for Dew Drop. "Have a fun ride!"

Singing from the top of their lungs, they sang their favorite song:

> *DEW DROP AND TOY*
> *HEARTS FILLED WITH JOY*
> *THEY SING SO HIGH*
> *THEY MADE THE VALLEY RING*
> *THEY SING SO HIGH*
> *CLEAR UP TO THE SKY*
> *AND THEY SING IN THE*
> *SWEET BYE AND BYE.*

How sweet their voices sounded to Mr. Warts. The girls gave him hope that there would be a brighter tomorrow.

*

Back in the shed the baby fox looked into the eyes of his mother. He could see how calm she was around the man who gave them shelter. The very day he was born he remembered how scared she was when a strange man almost found their home. She had always tried to teach him not to trust man. He didn't know why this man was different, but he trusted his mother.

She had always protected him and he knew she would until he was able to protect himself. He snuggled closer to his mother. The baby fox could feel the heat from her body. He just simply believed in her judgment and trusted her to do what was best for him and his sisters.

Walking home with Mr. Clagghorn, the girls were very quiet. They had a great deal to think about.

"What is wrong with you girls? I have never seen you two so quiet."

Raising her dark eyes to her brother, Dew Drop looked into his face. "Did you or Mr. Blew-it place an animal trap down by the old spring?"

"No! Why?"

"I was just wondering."

"Come on, Dew Drop; why would you ask such a question?"

"I'm not going to tell you unless you promise not to tell anyone."

"Tell what?"

"Do you promise?"

"Okay! I promise."

"Mr. Warts found a fox caught in a man-made trap down by the old spring. She had babies she was trying to protect. Why do people trap defenseless little animals like that?"

"Well, this is hard times for people and they sell their fur for money."

"What! You mean they kill them for their fur?"

"Think of it this way. We kill animals so we have something to eat. Killing a fox for its fur is almost the same thing. The money a person gets for the fur can buy food and clothes for the whole family. Do you understand?"

"No! I think its mean and I'm not going to eat any meat ever again."

"You won't tell anyone about the fox, will you?"

"I promised you I wouldn't tell and I won't!"

Dew Drop looked at her brother and she knew how lucky she was to have him for her very own brother.

Every day after school the girls would go see the fox. Dew Drop never told anyone about the fox. When Honey Bee would come around, she was real careful not to tell her. She had some hateful cousins and Dew Drop was worried they would hurt the fox. Some boys were just plain mean.

Saturday came too fast for the girls. They knew the fox would be better off in the forest, but they had grown attached to the beauty and her babies.

"Well, Mr. Warts, I guess it's time to set her free."

Looking into the eyes of the mother fox, Dew Drop said, "Toy and I will remember you forever." Kneeling down by the wild fox, Dew Drop touched the babies' soft fur. They squirmed closer to their mother but they didn't seem frightened. Their fur felt like it was alive with fire and warmth.

"Soft as a baby kitten," whispered Dew Drop.

All of a sudden the door to the shed was pushed open with a thud. Mr. Warts turned around to look into the face of the intruders.

"What are you boys doing here?" The mother fox growled and showed her big teeth.

"Get out! You are not welcome here," shouted Dew Drop.

The big boys held baseball bats and were swinging them around trying to scare them. Dew Drop placed her body over the babies to protect them. Toy started to cry and yelled, "Leave us alone!"

"We don't want to hurt anyone, but we do want that fox and her babies. She belongs to us anyway. We caught her in our traps."

Mr. Warts started moving slowly backwards. He wanted to get some leverage by surprising them from behind.

Dew Drop, hiding the babies with her body, was determined not to move. "You boys are going to be in big trouble for trapping on our land. Daddy Waggs would never allow you to put animal traps where someone could get hurt."

"Move little girl or you will get hurt!"

"I DON'T BELIEVE YOU BOYS ARE GOING TO HURT ANYONE!"

Looking into the eyes of John, the boys started to back away. Whining, they started to speak but John didn't give them a chance.

"You boys are on private property. NOW GET OUT AND DON'T COME BACK!"

Grabbing the back of the biggest boy's collar he said, "If you ever place another trap on my land again, I will call the sheriff and have you thrown in jail. DO I MAKE MYSELF CLEAR?"

"Yes."

"I CAN'T HEAR YOU!!"

"YES, SIR."

"Be gone with you and take your worthless friends with you."

Daddy Waggs looked at the girls and with the same gruffness said, "I thought I told you girls that you could not come here by yourselves. Now get home and I'll deal with you later!"

The girls hurried past their father and took one last look at the fox and her babies. The mother fox felt trapped and was worried for her little ones.

Mr. Warts looked at Daddy Waggs and was very grateful for his appearance. Mr. Warts was very upset because he knew the girls could have been seriously hurt.

John looked into Mr. Warts' eyes and said, "The girls are not to come back here without an escort. Do you understand me? I am going to have to make

sure this doesn't happen again. You probably won't
see them for at least a month."

"John! How did you know they were here?"

"Honey Bee came by the farm and told us her
cousins were going to your place to get a fox. She
was worried and wanted us to stop them. I was
panic stricken when I found out the girls were over
here."

"Mr. Warts, I advise you to let that fox go. Be
careful and have a good day."

"Come on, boys. Let's go home. We have work
to do!"

Mr. Warts watched the three of them walk off
toward the big farm-house. He was really glad to
see John and his sons. He could have given a good
account of himself, but he knew he would have lost
the battle.

The girls walked to the house with a heavy heart.
They were wondering what kind of punishment
they were going to get. They really didn't do
anything wrong. Daddy Waggs was so furious and

they will probably get a spanking.

Reaching the porch, the girls saw their mother standing by the screen door. Toy broke down and started to cry.

"Oh, Mum, it was awful. Those mean boys were going to hurt that defenseless little fox and her babies."

"What about you girls?"

"No, we aren't hurt and neither did Daddy Waggs and the boys get hurt. You should have seen them send those boys running off like scared rabbits."

Opening the screen door, Mum hugged the little girls close to her heart. She was so glad to see them. "Go to your room and wash the dirt off your faces."

Dew Drop and Toy hurried up the stairs and Dew Drop wiped the tears from Toy's eyes.

"We have to tell Daddy Waggs how brave he was," said Dew Drop. "If we tell him how strong he is, and tell him how great he is; maybe we won't get spanked. We will butter him up a lot, and tell him

how much we love him…and give him a big hug.
What do you think, Toy?"

"I think we had better keep our mouths shut and
just hope for the best."

"Toy, you are so sweet. Just trust me and I'll
take care of everything."

John and the boys were finishing up their work
in the barn. "Thank you boys for telling me about
the fox. I knew those girls were up to something,
but I didn't know what! We were all pretty scared.
Those girls are always getting into trouble."

Daddy Waggs looked at the boys and said, "I
believe those girls are about to get their angel wings
clipped."

Daddy Waggs walked on the porch and yelled,
"WHERE ARE YOU GIRLS?"

"Now John," said Sweet Pearl.

John looked at his wife and said, "Get supper on
the table and we will be right there."

The two girls came down the stairs and looked
into the face of their furious father.

Dew Drop started to speak but her father said, "BE QUIET! I don't want to hear anything from you. It is my turn to talk and I want you to go outside and pick a switch off the birch tree. NOW!"

Their hearts hammering in their chest, the girls did what they were told. The girls walked inside with their switch. Toy was crying and tried to hold back her tears.

Dew Drop looked at her father and he said to her, "Don't give me those black eyes! You are responsible for this." Dew Drop mumbled something under her breath.

"WHAT DID YOU SAY?"

"I said I can't help it if my eyes are black. That's their color; black that is…You always say, don't give me those black eyes and I can't help it."

"Are you trying to make me angry?"

"No! I was just trying to explain my eyes."

"BE QUIET!"

"Toy, stop that crying! I haven't touched you yet. Sit down and eat your supper!"

The girls sat down on the bench. Daddy Waggs came over and laid the switch on the bench between them. The girls swallowed hard and the food they were eating tasted like dust.

"May we be excused?" said Dew Drop.

"Both of you girls go upstairs and wait for me. I will be up shortly," said Daddy Waggs.

Gulping back tears, Toy could hardly make her feet move.

"Don't worry, Toy. I will take your punishment for you," said Dew Drop.

"Let me tell you a secret, Toy! Daddy Waggs wants everyone to think he is a grizzly bear, but deep down inside he is only a teddy bear."

"Do you really think so?"

Turning around they saw a big shadow. Oh, No! Their Daddy was right behind them.

"I...I... I was just trying to make Toy feel better," stuttered Dew Drop.

Walking into their bedroom, their father closed the door behind them.

"Let's talk about your lies and deceit."

"What lies and deceit? We never tell lies and we never hurt anyone either," cried Dew Drop.

"Let's talk about how you never hurt anyone. First of all, you and Toy could have gotten seriously hurt today. Those boys were ready to hurt anyone who got in their way. You hurt my feelings and your mother's when you disobeyed."

"We have rules to keep you out of trouble," continued Daddy Waggs. We don't make up rules to hurt you. We just want to protect you from harm. We love you, but we cannot have you disobeying us every time you decide you know better than we do."

"We are your parents and we have the right to decide what is best for you. Do you understand me?"

"Yes, Daddy!"

Shaking their heads up and down, the girls let the tears roll down their cheeks.

"We are sorry, Daddy Waggs, and we will do better the next time," said Dew Drop.

"I'm glad you're sorry, but being sorry doesn't always make things better. I want you to know that you cannot sweet talk me out of punishing you. You were wrong and you must be punished."

Dew Drop moved closer to her father and said, "I will take Toy's punishment for her because this was all my fault."

"Come here, Toy. I want to talk to you." He stretched out his arms and Toy ran into them as fast as her little legs could carry her. He held her close to his heart. She laid her head on his chest and he wiped her tears with his hanky.

"Toy, did you know that going to see Mr. Warts without your brother was wrong?"

Shaking her head, she said in a small voice, "yes."

"Well, I have a problem. Both of you admit to disobeying me. What do you think I should do?"

Toy looked into the face of her father and the fear seemed to fade away. Her father was special and he always tried to do what was best for them.

Toy said to her daddy, "We did a bad thing. We don't want to be bad, but sometimes it just happens."

Her daddy released her from his embrace. He stood up to his full height and looked down at the girls. "There will not be anymore warnings. Every day after school, Dew Drop will help her mother with the chores. There will be no excuses. Toy can help her with the baby sitting during the day. After supper every night, you will spend the rest of the evening in your room. Your punishment will continue for a whole month. You will not see Mr. Warts for two months. I am sorry to be so harsh, but you girls will learn to obey."

"We will be good. You'll see," said Dew Drop.

"That remains to be seen. I'm going to leave that birch switch here just as a reminder of your promise to be good. Remember you promised me you will do your very best, and that's all I can ask."

The girls thought it would be easier to get a spanking. Two months without seeing Mr. Warts was a long time. Poor Mr. Warts was being punished right along with them.

I guess when we disobey, we do hurt other people, they thought.

#

Later that night, a shadow appeared in the girls' room. Toy opened her eyes for just a second and then drifted off to sleep. In her sleep, she thought the candy-colored sandman had visited their room again. He bent down and whispered, *"Go to sleep everything will be all right."*

John leaned his head against the closed door. Today was a day he would remember for years to come. He closed his eyes and saw Dew Drop covering the frightened babies with her little body. He saw Toy trusting him to hold her and keep her safe even in his anger. He saw the fear in his boys' eyes when they were running to grab a shovel and a pitchfork to protect their little sisters.

John raised his head and saw his Sweet Pearl looking into his face. She knew so much about him and she still loved him. How much better could life be? His wife and children were a gift from God. With all these special gifts, Daddy Waggs and Sweet Pearl were wealthy indeed.

CHAPTER 8

RUNNING SCARED

The weeks were long for the little girls but it was longer for Mr. Warts. He waited all winter for spring to arrive and bring new life to the barren valley. The trees were in bloom and their flowers gave off a fragrance unlike any perfume that man could create.

He heard rumors that John's father had sold some of the land to The Franklin Coal Mine. Nannyglow was a coal mining town since the early 1900's.

Strip mining, strips the land of its beauty and leaves the animals without a home. Mr. Warts thought of the fox and her babies. He had seen her many times since the spring thaw. She had made her home around the old shed that gave her comfort.

Shaking his head from all his memories, he walked very slowly back to his cottage. He was a lonely man with only his memories to keep him company. He missed the girls very much.

*

"Wake up, Dew Drop!"

Dew Drop just lay on her bed and barely moved.

"What's wrong with you? Are you sick?"

"No! I was just thinking about Grandpa."

"What about Grandpa?"

"I heard Daddy Waggs telling Mum that Grandpa sold some of our land to a dirty old coal mining company."

"Why did he do that?"

"I heard Daddy Waggs say that Grandpa needed the money. Daddy Waggs didn't seem very happy about it, but there was nothing that he could do."

Dew Drop sat up in bed and said, "Everyone talks about money. You would think it is the most important thing in the whole world. I just don't understand grown-ups. I never want to grow up and choose money over my family. Never! I think Grandpa is being mean."

Toy looked at Dew Drop and said, "What is
going to happen to the forest animals when they
clear away all the trees and dig up the ground?"

"I don't know but we have to find a way to help
them."

"Hurry, girls! Breakfast is ready," said Mum.
This was the last day of school and Dew Drop
wanted to wear her very best dress.

"Just think, Toy. Next year you can go to school
with me."

"Do you like school, Dew Drop?"

Looking at her sister, Dew Drop said, "of course
I do. Mrs. Wicks is real nice."

Dew Drop finished dressing and took one last
look at herself in the mirror. Smiling her approval,
Dew Drop took her old shoes and slipped them on
her feet. She couldn't help thinking how ugly they
were. Oh well! At least she had shoes to wear.

Hurrying down the stairs they saw Claude de
Ball sitting in a high chair eating his breakfast. He
was laughing at Mr. Blew-it and smeared oatmeal

all over his face. Angry, Mr. Blew-it stumbled up the stairs and slammed the door to his room. He was mumbling under his breath the whole way to his room. Mr. Blew-it had a temper and right now he wasn't in any mood for cleaning oatmeal off his face.

Daddy Waggs had already left for work. He was getting in more hours of work each day. Sweet Pearl sat down with the children and Toy was asked to say the blessing.

GOD IS GREAT! GOD IS GOOD. LET US THANK HIM FOR OUR FOOD! AMEN!

Oatmeal was dished out and Dew Drop couldn't help but notice that Sweet Pearl looked pale and tired.

"Are you all right, Mum? You look kind of sick."

Mum looked at Dew Drop and said, "I'm just fine. I guess I'm just a little tired. I will need Toy to help me with her baby brother while I finish the washing and the ironing."

Toy looked at her brother and frowned. Claude de Ball was so spoiled and he wanted all of her attention.

Mr. Blew-it, Mr. Clagghorn and Dew Drop started off to school. They hadn't gotten very far when they heard and saw the big heavy equipment coming up their lane.

Daddy Waggs had warned them to stay away from the mining operation. All the children knew how dangerous it could be. Even Dew Drop and Toy were going to obey this time. The strip mining will take place at the top of the mountain. They had to clear away the trees first. That means that the shelter for the animals will be destroyed.

The children were in deep thought as they walked to school. Dew Drop was thinking about helping those poor animals. She didn't have a plan yet, but she would do something. Mr. Blew-it was thinking how many changes had taken place since people had lost their jobs. This used to be a fun place to live but now everyone worried about how they were going to feed their families. This strip mining operation was going to give men a job for a good long time.

Mr. Clagghorn had a secret and he was afraid someone would find out about it. He would secretly go up the mountain and give a sermon to the forest animals. He knew he would be a preacher someday.

How was he going to explain to them why they were losing their homes? He named them all and they stood perfectly still when he told them about how much God loved them. He had to do something, but what? All the way to school he prayed that God would help him to know what to do. God loves animals too, doesn't He?

*

Back in the woods the animals were running scared.

"Hurry…Hurry…Run Children Run! I can't move any faster!"

Her feet pounding the ground as fast as she could, Mrs. Grey Heel, the rabbit, was trying to reach her children before the ground gave way and swallowed them whole.

Hairy O'Dor and his wife, Whiffal, were hovering over their babies trying to protect them from the monster who had destroyed their home. The baby skunks didn't know what was happening. The ground just shook and began to break away.

The trees were falling down with a thud—one after another. Flye-Bye the mother squirrel was out with her small family teaching them to gather nuts, and how to find food for their hungry little bellies. "TIMBER," cried a human. Fear in their hearts, the babies watched as their home had fallen to the ground. "Why mother, we don't understand?"

WHUSH! WHUSH! The big blade on the tractor just missed Two-Step the ground hog. Angry, the ground hog huffed and puffed and stood on its hind legs, shaking his fist at the green monster. "This is my home! Leave me alone!" The monster headed toward him again. "Oh!…Oh! You make me so mad!"

Two-Step had to run as fast as his fat legs would carry him. He lost the battle, and he lost his home. How could this be happening, he thought? Just a few hours ago he was playing with his friends.

Shaking with fear, Whimper, the deer and her fawn watched as the forest was being destroyed. The little fawn looked into the brown eyes of her mother. With expression in her eyes, she spoke one word, "WHY?"

All the animals' hearts were racing with fear. They all had questions that for the present had no answers.

The birds were squawking and crying to their mates! "Fly away! DANGER! We must escape!"

Mr. Blue Jay covered his mate with his out-spread wings. Crooning soft words in her ear, he said, "Don't worry everything will be okay." His words did nothing to soothe the frightened bird.

Looking at the fallen tree, she noticed the broken shell. Her babies would have hatched soon. Now they will never breathe life.

Flagger the mole was in his home and covered his wife and children with his body. His heart was beating like a drum. There wasn't enough time to say his goodbyes. The giant wheels crushed his bones and killed his crying family.

Flurry the fox ran as fast as he could to get away from the fallen trees. His fox hole was destroyed, but he was so grateful that his family was out searching for food. They would have never survived if they had been inside. He had to go and look for them. Where will they go? The whole mountain was coming down.

Dinger the porcupine and his wife were in the field when they saw the earth shatter around them. Running as fast as their bodies could go, they reached the top of the hill. They made it! Turning around at the loud noise behind them, a huge scoop shovel picked them up with the dirt. They couldn't breathe and they were preparing for the worst. Just when they thought all was lost, they were set down on the ground with a thud. "ESCAPE!" They were running for their lives. "Don't give up now! Keep on running!" The constant thud of the heavy wheels were a reminder of their fate.

When the children arrived home from their last day of school, they couldn't believe their eyes. A road was made to go through the mountain and up a big incline. Huge machines were pulling trees down the hill. The top of the mountain was nothing but a huge pile of dirt.

The birds were squawking loudly, and the animals were howling a shrill sound. Dew Drop and Toy began to shiver. They had chill bumps all over their body.

"OH! NO!" What has happened to all my friends? Mr. Clagghorn groaned.

Mr. Blew-it was stunned to see the destruction of property and fear gripped his heart for the animals.

"Mum, Mum, where are you?" cried all the children.

The girls were crying with great big tears rolling down their cheeks. Mum pulled them into her arms and held them while they cried. She knew what was coming. Mum knew that when the kids got home they would be broken-hearted.

The girls were still crying when Daddy Waggs walked into the kitchen. He looked at the boys with a worried look in his eyes.

"I'm sorry, kids! I don't own the land, but I did what I could. I gave my dad advice, but Grandpa had to do what he thought was best for all of us and for community. He thought he was doing the right thing and who is to say that he didn't."

The children gave their father a disgusted look. They were about to speak when he looked at them and said, "this isn't any of your business and we will never discuss the strip mining again."

It looked hopeless and the children ran upstairs to their rooms. What could they do? They were so upset that they didn't want to eat supper. Their father insisted they sit at the table anyway. The kids couldn't eat a bite. The food was tasteless and stuck to the roof of their mouths.

Daddy Waggs could see the children from the corner of his eye as he was loading his plate with more potatoes. He spoke with a gruff voice. "You kids better eat so you have the energy to help me round up the homeless animals. The way I have it figured, we could take them to the southwest corner of the farm. There is a beautiful spring-fed lake and plenty of trees. We use to think of it as the most beautiful part of the farm."

The children thought they were hearing things. They looked up from their plates and stared at their father. He winked at them and started eating again.

"Do you mean it?" they all said at once.

Laughing, Daddy Waggs said, "I never say anything I don't mean. Hurry up so we can get started."

The children ate with gusto and for some reason the food tasted real good.

Mr. Clagghorn stood at the top of the hill. He took out his homemade flute and whistled out a tune. The animals started coming out of their hiding places. Shaking his head, Mr. Blew-it couldn't believe that his brother could round them up so fast.

The rabbits, squirrels, raccoons, ground hogs, porcupines, foxes, deer, and skunks all came running at the soft sound. Even the birds flew overhead to follow the little boy with a sing-song voice.

"Don't be afraid. Follow us! My family will help you find a peaceful place to live. I have never lied to you before...Come!"

Dew Drop and Toy picked up some of the little ones and helped them to cross the wide farm. Daddy Waggs and Mr. Blew-it helped them cross the wide ravine to the little valley.

The sun was going down and the sky had turned a little darker blue. Streaks of pink and orange spread across the blue sky. Mr. Clagghorn had stood in front of the fading sun. He looked like he was on fire. The animals stood in awe of the handsome little boy. He spoke with a clear voice and said,

"This is your new home. This property belongs to my father and you can live here in peace for as long as you desire."

The animals were spell-bound. They all started to chatter all at once. Even the crickets joined the happy singing and chatter. There were more trees than they needed. The little valley had a richness that couldn't be described.

The animals had lost their homes but God had provided a better and more beautiful place to live. This was better then they could have ever dreamed. They were so grateful to have another chance.

Everyone was quiet on their way home. They were thinking about how everything was provided for the homeless animals. Daddy Waggs thought about his own life. God had given him and Sweet Pearl all the provisions they ever needed. Someday maybe they would build a home in that little valley. He had almost forgotten about it until he asked God to help him find a solution that would make his children happy again.

#

Later that night the shadow appeared in their room again. The girls couldn't wake up enough to see who was there. He walked over to the bed, bent down and whispered in their ear. It must be the candy-colored sandman for he sprinkled star dust and whispered, *"Go to sleep. Everything will be all right."*

John closed the door and went to his room with joy and peace in his heart. He thanked God for helping him come up with the right solution for his heart-broken children.

CHAPTER 9

THE ANGRY BEAR

The animals in the valley made a promise to each other. They decided they would go outside of the valley to find their food. Everyone was like family and even the fox searched for its food outside of the little paradise.

Just like every paradise, there is always something to destroy its beauty. The heavy rains brought mudslides from the mountain. The little animals quaked and shivered with fear.

Dew Drop and Toy would go to the valley as often as possible. They loved to play hide and seek with the animals. Toy was still a little afraid but she was beginning to learn to trust them a little at a time.

The girls would visit Mr. Warts and he would happily go with them. The animals learned to trust him and he would sit for hours telling them stories

115

of adventure. They all worked together to keep the valley beautiful.

Dew Drop and Toy told their father about the mudslides in the valley. Mr. Blew-it and Mr. Clagghorn worked with their father to dig trenches around the valley. Daddy Waggs had told the mine workers about the mudslides. They used their equipment to dig ditches around the valley so the mud wouldn't slide into the valley.

Everything seemed to be just about perfect. The little Blue Jay had built another nest and had four little eggs she was protecting. Two-Step the groundhog was happy with his new home and it was even better than the old one.

It was time for the sun to find for its resting place. It started to fall down behind the mountain with bright streaks of red and lavender spreading across the sky.

The night was quiet and the only sounds were the sound of bull frogs and crickets singing their songs of joy.

Two big blood-shot eyes watched the sleepy little valley. No one knew of his presence, but he knew about them. He was watching, always watching, for the right moment to attack. This was a chance of a lifetime and he didn't want to ruin it by being in a hurry.

The next morning the girls did their chores and asked permission to go see Mr. Warts. Mr. Clagghorn took them over to the cottage but Mr. Warts wasn't there.

"Where do you think he is?" asked the girls. Mr. Clagghorn shook his head and started to walk back to the farm.

Honey Bee was walking toward them and with non-stop chatter started to talk to the girls.

"Did you hear about the big black bear that is circling the woods? My dad said it is the biggest bear he has ever seen!"

"Your dad saw the bear?" said Mr. Clagghorn. Mr. Clagghorn knew that Honey Bee exaggerated her stories most of the time.

"Well, he only saw the bear tracks, but he said that the bear has to weigh at least two thousand pounds."

Mr. Clagghorn looked at the girls and said, "We better hurry and get back to the farm. I bet Daddy Waggs doesn't know about this."

Dew Drop cried, "Do you think Mr. Warts is all right?"

"Dew Drop! Stop making trouble where there isn't any. I'm sure Mr. Warts probably went to Nannyglow for some supplies."

Toy looked at her brother and said, "You think you know everything?"

Honey Bee laughed at Toy's remark. Toy looked at Honey Bee and said, "What's so funny?"

"I think you are, and the funny part is you don't even know it."

Just as Toy was going to make a remark, the kids heard a loud growl that shook the ground. "We better hurry and get home. Mum will be getting worried about us, and right now I am beginning to worry myself," said Mr. Clagghorn.

Running as fast as they could the children tripped over each other trying to get home. Big blood-shot eyes watched as the children ran farther away from his den. They were pretty close but not quite close enough. Someday he would get them all!

"Mum! Mum!" cried the girls. "Where are you, Mum?"

Sweet Pearl was rocking Claude de Ball to sleep.

"Hush, the baby is almost asleep."

Laying the baby in his bed, Mum kissed him and closed the bedroom door.

"What's all the noise?" she asked.

We heard a big bear and we think he was chasing us.

Mum looked at the children and said, "I think you kids have a big imagination."

The kids looked at their mother and thought she didn't look like she felt very well.

Honey Bee started to tell her everything she knew when Mr. Clagghorn stopped her.

"I think we might have imagined it, don't you think girls?"

Toy looked at her brother and thought he had completely lost his mind. Dew Drop reached up and held her hands over Toy's mouth.

Struggling to get loose, Toy heard her sister say, "We had better get going and make sure Honey Bee gets home okay."

Leaving the house, the girls looked at each other and thought they had better keep silent about the bear. They would never be allowed to go anywhere. Yes, silence was the best thing.

While the girls thought they were keeping a big secret, Daddy Waggs and Mr. Blew-it were at a town meeting discussing what could be done about the huge black bear.

Pounding his fist on the table, Mr. Yo-Yo yelled from the top of his lungs. "We have to do something as soon as possible! We can't let that bear stop our mining operations! We are losing money every day that bear is out there. He is destroying everything in its path."

Daddy Waggs looked at Mr. Yo-Yo and said, "I think you are doing a good job of doing that!"

"Are we going to call each other names or are we going to band together and get that bear?"

"You're right! I shouldn't have lashed out at you. I am just worried for my family," said Daddy Waggs.

Mr. Jaggs, who was foreman at the mine said, "I think we can use our backhoe and dig us a big pit to trap the bear."

"Well, it's worth a try," said the men.

Leaving the town hall the men started to go home when they heard a loud growl. The ground trembled and the men were awe-struck at the sound.

"You better make that a deep pit, Jaggs!"

Reaching home, Daddy Waggs called his family together and told them about the bear.

"I do not want to see anyone going beyond our barn. No one will venture out of the main yard. Do I make myself clear?"

"Yes, we will stay close to the house," said the children.

Daddy Waggs looked at his family and said, "We are up against a huge bear and I don't know what will happen."

The newspapers were carrying the story of the big bear. One man had reported seeing it and he said it was the biggest bear that ever appeared in this area. God help them all when that bear decides to strike.

The little valley was making its own plans to protect themselves from the huge bear. The birds were flying around letting the animals know when the bear was in the area.

They would all go deep into the woods and hide until the birds let them know the coast was clear. The bear was amused at the efforts they made. He knew he could get them all if he chose to do it.

He was bored with the human efforts, also. The humans were running around trying to make his life miserable. He had to admit that he growled as loud as he could just to scare them. He was tired and bored and he knew it was time to make his anger known to all.

That evening the children were in the barn feeding the animals. The moon was full and the wind was blowing and howling. Dew Drop stayed as close as she could to Mr. Blew-it.

"Dew Drop, I don't need a shadow," said Mr. Blew-it.

"I can't help it! I have the feeling someone or something is watching us."

The boys laughed and finished their chores.

Mr. Clagghorn said, "I think everyone is in a panic over nothing. That bear is probably bored and left the area already. We haven't heard him in a long time." They all hoped he was right, but Mr. Blew-it was sure that the bear was still around.

The children fastened the barn door shut and started toward the house. Dew Drop was glad they were finished with their chores. She didn't like going out to the barn anymore.

Toy was watching out the window waiting for the kids to return. The moon was bright and she could see them closing the barn door. She was worried until she saw them heading toward the house.

Hurry! She thought. *I love you and I want you in the house safe.*

The men in the village were making plans to rid themselves of the bear. They all were carrying torches and rifles and had plans of backing the bear into the huge pit that was dug just for him.

The pit was dug not far from the mining operations. They were headed into that direction when they heard children screaming. Panic stricken, John knew that his children were in danger.

The terrible sounds of screaming children and monster growls from the bear brought everyone running to the barnyard. Horror and escalating fear such as they have never known before; the children stood face to face with a giant bear.

Mr. Blew-it pushed the children behind him and

told them to walk very slowly to the house. "Do not run! Now Go!"

Crying, the children yelled, "we can't leave you by yourself."

"Don't argue with me, Mr. Clagghorn take Dew Drop to the house! NOW!!"

The children walked backwards to the house. They didn't take their eyes off the bear. Mum and Toy stood at the window in horror as they watched Mr. Blew-it face down the bear.

The men were still too far away to help him. Mr. Blew-it looked into the black eyes of the monster bear. He just knew that this was going to be his last day on earth.

"Well, Mr. Bear, it looks like it's just me and you. I know you could kill me with just one swipe of your huge paw."

The bear was mildly amused at the little human who stood before him. He was brave. He had to give him points for that. The bear moved closer and watched the young man tremble with fear.

Looking up at the bear, Mr. Blew-it said in as loud of a voice as he could, "YOU ARE REALLY SOMETHING! I HOPE YOU CAN SLEEP AT NIGHT AFTER SCARING EVERYONE HALF TO DEATH. AS FAR AS I CAN TELL, YOU HAVEN'T EVEN HURT ONE ANIMAL OR HUMAN IN THIS WHOLE AREA. WE KNOW WE DISTURBED YOUR HOME AND YOU ARE ANGRY. LOOK AROUND YOU! THOSE MEN HAVE THEIR RIFLES POINTED AT YOU."

The bear could sense other humans and he knew that he couldn't get them all before they got him. Standing to his full height, the bear growled with such authority that the men trembled in their shoes.

Mr. Blew-it stood his ground and never moved. He waited to see what the bear was going to do. The animals in the little valley were watching the scene take place. This was it—the showdown of all times. The men with their rifles ready to fire...Mr. Blew-it praying that the bear would just give up...the animals fearful of it all, waited for the final ending.

126

The big bear dropped down on all four feet, shook his massive head and turned around and walked away toward the woods. His angry growl shook the trees and even the ground trembled.

The men all rushed up to Mr. Blew-it and patted him on his back.

"That was the best eye-stalking we have ever seen," said the men.

John looked into the eyes of his son and said, "I am so very proud of you. You have saved us all from a terrible disaster."

Just as John put his arm around his son, Mr. Blew-it crumbled to the ground. John picked him up in his arms and carried him to the house.

The children all huddled around him as Daddy Waggs laid him on the couch.

"Give the boy some room," he said.

Tears rolling down their cheeks, the girls hugged him and slapped wet kisses on his cheeks. Wiping his face Mr. Blew-it said, "That's enough! Stop it!" The children laughed and cried at the same time.

Sweet Pearl had cried a few tears of her own. She kissed her son and hugged her children close to her heart. The whole evening was filled with chatter and great joy. The growls of the bear were heard throughout the whole village. Everyone stayed on alert for the night. No one knew what the bear would do next.

The bear felt a force of something pushing him toward the other side of the mountain. He knew that for the present time he was defeated. That little brave human had defeated him. He also knew that he would get another chance some day.

#

That night John looked at his children as they slept. Tears filled his eyes as he was reminded again of how wonderful his children are. They are gifts from an almighty God and loving them was the easiest thing he has ever done. They tried his patience at every turn, but it was worth it.

CHAPTER 10

THE VOICE OF ANGELS

Kicking and screaming, Toy was awakened from her nightmare. Sweat running down her face she woke up with a startled cry. Toy looked over at Dew Drop who was sound asleep. She looked like an angel sleeping in a peaceful dreamland. How could she sleep when I am having nightmares? Toy thought.

Toy laid back down and pulled the covers over her head. She tried very hard to remember her nightmare, but she could not remember a thing. Slowly she drifted off to sleep.

The ground was covered with dew and a haze of smoke-like mist filled the air like a cloudy vapor. Trying to find the pretty lady through the smoke, Toy started to follow her again.

"Where are you?" cried Toy! I know you are there I can faintly see you."

Struggling to find her, Toy followed deeper and deeper into the haze of smoke. Twisting and turning Toy searched for the lady, but she disappeared once again.

"Come back I think I know you!"

Once again she disappeared into the thin air. Attempting to return from where she started, Toy couldn't find her way back home. The smoke was heavier and she had trouble seeing through it.

Drifting back from her dream, Toy looked into the face of Dew Drop.

"What's wrong? I heard you crying out!"

Toy still could not remember her dream.

"I just had a nightmare. Go back to sleep."

Dew Drop went back to her bed and it didn't take long for her to go back to sleep. Toy lay in her bed with her eyes wide open.

Bright and early the next morning the girls looked out their window and noticed a flock of blackbirds in the back yard. The ground was plowed and ready for planting. The birds were fighting over the worms that had surfaced.

"I can't believe all that noise for just a few worms," said Dew Drop.

"Sometimes we fight over things that to some people seem just as silly," said Toy.

"My, my! Aren't we happy today!"

Toy looked at her sister and said, "I didn't get much sleep last night. Something or someone kept me from sleeping."

"Maybe you were still thinking about that stupid old bear."

"No! That wasn't it. I must have been dreaming about a fire because all I can remember is a lot of smoke."

Dew Drop looked at her sister and said, "What kind of fire are you talking about?"

"That's just it! I can't remember."

"Well, we have to go and see Mr. Warts today. Maybe he can help us figure out your dream."

After breakfast dishes were done, Mr. Clagghorn took the girls over to Mr. Warts' cottage. They looked all around, but he wasn't there. Dew Drop looked into the brown eyes of her brother and said, "You don't think the bear got him, do you?"

Mr. Clagghorn laughed and said, "You're a silly goose. Mr. Blew-it and I saw him just yesterday planting his garden."

"Don't make fun of me. We haven't seen him for a long time."

"Who haven't you seen for a long time?"

Turning around, the girls saw a little man who was all bent over. His face was more wrinkled and his hands were twisted with pain. He looked really old, but his face beamed with joy.

The girls were so excited to see Mr. Warts that they ran into his waiting arms. He hugged them a little harder than he should have, and held them close to his heart.

"Oh, Mr. Warts! We missed you so much," said Dew Drop.

"I missed you girls, too! Let's go inside and get some cookies. I just bought some today."

Mr. Clagghorn left the girls in good hands and walked back to the farm. He was laughing as he thought about the wild imagination they both had. I feel sorry for Mr. Warts, he thought. He was old and sometimes sly like a fox. He could tell those girls story after story and they would believe every word he said.

Laughing, he said, "Good luck, Mr. Warts."

Mr. Warts was swinging them on the swing he made for them. They were swinging higher and higher, and singing louder and louder. The clouds were so white and fluffy and it brought back a deep desire to float on them again.

When they were done swinging, the girls wondered why they thought they could float on those clouds. They had only done that once and it was in a dream. Dew Drop looked at Toy and asked Mr. Warts if he knew anything about dreams.

Mr. Warts laughed and said, "dreams are very special and only special people have them."

"We have them Mr. Warts, are we special?"

"Of course you are special! I should know because I am the dream maker of all times."

Toy looked at Mr. Warts and said with all the hope in her heart, "I have dreams about a white mist and smoke all around me. I can't find my way out of the smoke. There is something else, but I can't remember what it is. What do you think?"

Scratching his head, he said, "I have to think about that. Maybe you were seeing a place that only exists in your mind. This is a mystery but don't you worry, we will get to the bottom of it."

The girls played for hours and went to the little valley with Mr. Warts. They couldn't remember how long it had been since they laughed so much.

Hairy O'Dor the skunk, Flye-Bye the squirrel, and Harper the chipmunk all came to play. Flurry the fox brought his friends with him along with Two-Step the ground hog. They were all happy and chattering to their hearts' content.

Mr. Clagghorn came to the valley looking for them. "I have been looking for you everywhere.

It's time to go home. We have to hurry!"

The girls waved good-bye to everyone and headed back to the farm. "What's wrong?"

"We have chores to do and Mum was sick. Daddy Waggs had sent Mr. Blew-it to get the doctor."

Everything centered around their mother. She was the one who made each day happy. The whole house was gloomy without her.

The doctor arrived and said she was going to be all right. She had to rest more every day. Mouths dropped opened when the doctor said that she was going to have a baby.

"A BABY!"

"We can't have another baby!"

Laughing at the kids' reaction, the doctor said, "Well, you have no choice. God has given this family another gift."

Shocked at the news, everyone had their own idea about what a gift was. A baby was not on their gift list.

Stunned at the news himself, Daddy Waggs walked off the porch and headed for the barn. He had work to do, and of course, he had some planning to do. Shaking his head, his mind wondered back to the time his first-born was brought into the world. They had five children and was about to have another. Oh—my! What was he going to do?

The beautiful summer days were flying by too quickly for the girls. They helped their mother every day with the chores and watched Claude de Ball when their mother rested.

Dew Drop and Toy would rather be outside playing with the animals in the valley. They tried not to complain but it was hard to keep their feelings to themselves. Some of their animal friends would come looking for them.

Where are those two little humans, thought Whimper the Deer. Flurry the fox, Dinger the porcupine, and Gray Heel the rabbit watched as Dew Drop and Toy carried a noisy, chubby, pumpkin-face little boy to the porch. They put him in a wooden play area and he started to pucker his face to cry.

Trying to get their attention, the animals stood on their hind legs and squealed. The girls turned around and laughed with delight. Dew Drop waved at them and welcomed them with a smile.

"Hello! We have missed all of you so much. As you can see, we are babysitting our little brother."

"Isn't he cute?" Toy said with pride.

The animals all started chattering all at once. Laughing, the girls knew the animals were agreeing with Toy.

Claude de Ball laughed, and played, while the animals did cute little somersaults and chased each other. Babysitting couldn't have been easier this day. The girls would take turns running and playing with them. Before long it was mid-afternoon and time to take their brother inside for lunch and a nap.

"Come back and play with us again," said Dew Drop. "We had great fun today."

The animals stood on their hind legs and waved good-bye to their little friends.

Later that night while the girls were sleeping, Toy had another dream about the pretty lady dressed in white. This time she saw her face. Drifting into a deeper sleep, Toy could hear her voice. The voice was so soft and sweet, but she couldn't quite understand what she was saying.

A heavy white film of smoke filled Toy's dream. Steam from the ground lifted into the air, swirling into a funnel-like cloud. The lady drifted farther and farther away from Toy. A bright light appeared above her head and Toy could see a whole realm of ladies dressed in white.

They were singing and their voices were so soft and beautiful that Toy wanted to sing along with them. The voices quickly faded and the web-like smoke slowly disappeared.

"Wait! Don't go! Wait! Please wait!"

Startled, Toy awoke with her heart beating faster than it ever did before. She wasn't afraid! She just couldn't understand why she would dream about angels in heaven. Is that what she saw and heard? *"No! It can't be!"*

Dew Drop's chatter awoke Toy. "What did you say, Dew Drop?"

"Toy! What is wrong with you?"

"I said this is Sunday and I want to wear my new dress that Mum made for us. We can be dressed like twins today. Okay?"

"Sure, Dew Drop—whatever you want."

This Sunday was very hot and humid. The sweat was rolling down Daddy Waggs back. His mind was on his wife who was unable to attend church. She was pale and weak. This baby she was carrying took a lot of her strength and energy. The life was being drained right out of her. John was so worried he missed hearing the quiet voice of God.

The service seemed to last a long time. Everyone was glad when the last song was sung. A lady dressed in white sang the last song. Toy looked at her and listened to her sweet voice.

Soft as a voice of an angel, thought Toy. Toy had never seen her before. Who was she, and why did she happen to be here this Sunday?

All the way home, Toy was haunted by that voice. She looked at her brother, Mr. Clagghorn, and asked him if he ever saw an angel.

"Why would you ask such a question?"

"I was just curious," she said.

Looking at his sister, Mr. Clagghorn noticed how pale she was.

"You are really serious about angels, aren't you?"

"Oh just forget it!"

When they finally got home, the girls hurried to change out of their good clothes. Laughing and running up the stairs, they ran into Daddy Waggs coming out of his bedroom.

"Be quiet! Your mother needs her rest."

The girls looked at his worried face and walked very quietly into their room. Chattering and laughing they were unaware of the dark cloud that surrounded their home.

Aunt Free-da came to the house and offered to bring the children over to her house to play. Dew Drop and Toy knew that something was wrong.

Walking over to their aunt's house, their minds were working overtime. They knew Mum was sick and no one told them anything.

Aunt Free-da gave them dinner and the girls helped do the dishes. Claude de Ball was fed and rocked to sleep. Mr. Clagghorn and Mr. Blew-it brought some clothes for the children to spend the night.

"Why are we to stay for the night?" said Dew Drop.

They looked at Aunt Free-da and just said, "Daddy Waggs thought you would like a sleep over."

"We will have a lot of fun," said Aunt Free-da.

The girls looked at the boys and said, "Is Mum feeling better?"

Mr. Blew-it shook his head and said, "I'm sure

she is feeling better by now. Well, Mr. Clagghorn
and I better get home. We have work to do. See you
tomorrow, girls."

The girls were asking all kinds of questions and
really not getting any answers. Later that evening
when it was time to go to bed, Toy began to get
worried that she would see the angels again. Why
were they appearing before her? Were they trying to
tell her something? Don't be silly, she told herself.
She lay in her bed a long time before she finally
went to sleep.

It was another two days before the girls and their
baby brother went home. They had such a good
time that they hated to see it end. Kissing Aunt
Free-da good-bye, they pushed Claude de Ball
home in a buggy. Mr. Blew-it told them that Daddy
Waggs wanted to talk to them when they got home.

Hearts skipping a beat, they walked into the
kitchen and looked at Daddy Waggs. He reached
out his arms and asked them to climb up on his lap.
It was strange but they both fit perfect.

Toy put her little arm around her daddy's neck and light eyes looked into dark ones. Her little voice was quivering and she said, "Daddy, what can we do for you?" So sweet were his little girls. He loved them so very much.

"Daddy has something to tell you and I'm not sure how I can tell you."

Dew Drop looked into his dark eyes and smiled. "It's all right, Daddy. We promise not to cry very much."

"Your mother has been very ill and was not able to carry her child. He was too little and just couldn't survive. I'm sorry, girls."

Toy hugged her daddy's neck and said, "If he was too little to be born, would Jesus take him to heaven anyway?"

His arms tightened around their little bodies and tenderly he said, "I don't have all the answers. I do know that he had a beating heart. And with that beating heart, he had a soul that was crying out to be released to God."

The girls leaned their heads into their daddy's chest and softly cried.

"When your mother is feeling better, we will all go and see the grave where he is buried. He doesn't have a name yet, so we will have each of you choose a name and we will pick the one that best suits him."

The girls were as close to their daddy as they had ever been. They slipped off his lap and went upstairs to visit their mother. She greeted them with a smile and held them close to her heart.

"Are you okay, Mum? We were really worried about you."

Mum hugged them and said, "I feel fine and before long we will all be back to normal. Whatever that means," she said.

Laughing, they sat on the bed and talked to her for a long time.

The baby needed a name and the whole family was trying real hard to come up with just the right name. Saturday was the day that was chosen to say their final good-byes. Pastor Rob was going to speak at the graveside service. Friends and neighbors were coming to give the family their support.

Toy whispered into her daddy's ear so no one could hear her choice of names. She didn't want anyone to laugh at her.

"That's a great name, Toy. We will think about it."

She gave her daddy a hug and walked away with a big smile on her face.

The sun was setting and the clouds had moved low in the sky. They almost looked like they shadowed the mountains. Dew Drop and Toy said their prayers and climbed into bed. Tomorrow was going to be a strange day for them. They were going to say good-bye to a brother they never got to know.

Toy closed her eyes and heard voices calling to her. She sat up and with her eyes wide open she saw a cloud of smoke swirling around her. Whispering, she said, *"Who... are you?"*

"We are special angels sent by God to tell you that your baby brother is home in the arms of Jesus. There are a lot of little babies in heaven. Some of them died before they even breathed a breath of air. Don't worry about him and keep him always close to your heart."

The voices started to fade. Toy watched as they swirled and twisted around her bed. She looked around and saw herself still asleep in her bed. Slowly she saw her body floating down toward her bed. She heard a voice say, *"Baby Boy Roy was a great name, Toy! Goodnight."*

The family stood around the little grave that had a little stone cross. The name of Baby Boy Roy was written across the front. The friends and neighbors had already gone and only the family was left to say their last good-byes.

Dew Drop had no idea that she could feel so much love for a baby she didn't even know. They threw their flowers on the grave and started to walk away.

Mum had cried until there were no more tears left. Daddy Waggs didn't cry much. He just held his Sweet Pearl while she cried. Dew Drop cried for the brother she didn't know. Toy looked at the clear sky, and with tears rolling down her cheeks she whispered, *"Thank You!"*

The boys laid their flowers down on the hard ground. They each wondered what he would have looked like. Some day he might have been a doctor, or a musician, or a preacher, but it wasn't meant to be.

The family started to leave when they saw Mr. Warts and all the animals from the valley standing close by them. He hugged the girls and told them all how sorry he was for their loss. The place was quiet and seemed empty, but the sky looked brighter and clearer than it ever had before.

Toy knew in her heart that she would never see her angels again. Sometimes when she was alone, she could hear their voices and feel their presence. She had her very own guardian angel.

CHAPTER 11

ATTIC FRIENDS

Standing at the bottom of the long narrow staircase, the girls gulped back their fear and put one foot in front of the other. Honey Bee was first. After all, it was her aunt's attic.

"I told you girls there is nothing to be afraid of," said Honey Bee.

"It looks pretty scary to me," said Toy.

Dew Drop looked at Toy and gave her a big smile. "I'm sure everything will be all right, Toy."

"Come on you guys! I never thought you would be afraid of your own shadow."

Raising her chin to prove how brave she was, Dew Drop blurted out the words, "We are not afraid!"

Reaching the top of the stairs, Honey Bee reached for the door and pulled the cord on the light switch.

"Here we are!"

The attic was full of unwanted treasurers. There was a rocking horse with big brown eyes and long dark eyelashes sitting all by itself in the corner. The horse was pretty big with a homemade saddle on its back. Toy gave it a push so it would rock back and forth.

Looking around they saw a huge doll house with torn shutters and a chimney that was falling apart. The roof was tattered and the door hinges were broken.

"I bet this was a great house a long time ago," said Dew Drop.

The whole room was filled with broken dolls and moth eaten stuffed animals.

"I'm sure these toys were loved by someone a long time ago," said Toy.

The girls looked around and knew this attic was full of memories and forgotten dreams. A cream colored vase with huge handles on both sides sat on a table in the corner. Toy was drawn to the vase and picked it up to get a better look at it. A painted picture of a lady with a beautiful face and long blonde hair stared back at her.

"She is so beautiful," said Toy. Staring at the lady, Toy knew she had seen her somewhere before.

"Come here, Toy! Look at this," said Dew Drop.

Toy followed Dew Drop and looked at the rabbit standing in front of the small window. The rabbit had a missing ear and its nose had been chewed off. He looked happy in spite of his appearance.

Toy and Dew Drop fell in love with the poor rabbit. Honey Bee started to laugh when she looked at the rabbit.

"Look at that stupid rabbit. He's pretty ugly, don't you think?"

"No! You are so mean sometimes. He just needs someone to take care of him and love him," said Dew Drop.

"Aunt Dee Bee said we could choose any toy we wanted."

The girls looked at Honey Bee and couldn't

believe that someone would give them such a gift.

"Are you sure?" said Dew Drop.

"Of course, I'm sure. She told me that just the other day."

Looking around they saw broken dolls, broken dishes, skates, an old ball glove, and a chest of make-believe dress-up clothes and old shoes. We could play up here forever, thought the girls.

Dew Drop spotted a round pink box with a tiny ballerina girl on the top of the lid. She turned it up side down and turned the key. It played a soft tune. The little ballerina dressed in pink with tiny pink slippers, swayed and danced with the soft music.

So many treasures and they could only choose just one. Which one would they choose?

"Girls! It's time for lunch."

"We will be right there, Aunt Dee Bee!"

The girls shut the light off and closed the attic door. They walked down the long, narrow stairs and hurried to wash their hands.

Aunt Dee Bee smiled and said, "Did you girls

find something special in my attic?"

"Oh, yes! We found a lot of good stuff," said Dew Drop.

Aunt Dee Bee laughed and gave thanks to God for their food. The girls ate in silence. They wanted to ask Aunt Dee Bee about the toys in the attic, but they decided not to ask her. They were afraid that Honey Bee was wrong about choosing a gift. No one had ever given them anything before.

Aunt Dee Bee looked at Dew Drop and knew she had something on her mind.

"Why don't you girls come back tomorrow? You will have all night tonight to decide which toy you would like."

Toy looked into her eyes and smiled a big smile. "That is a great idea!"

Dew Drop said, "We want to thank you for letting us come here and for giving us a gift from your attic."

Aunt Dee Bee looked at the girls and said, "You misunderstood me."

Dew Drop's big black eyes looked at her. She knew it was too good to be true. She just knew it!

"The toy I give you isn't free."

"But...but we thought you were going to give it to us," cried Toy.

"We have no money," said Dew Drop.

Aunt Dee Bee looked at the sad faces of the girls and said, "I'm sorry, but your toy comes with a higher price than money."

The girls looked shocked.

"Money will not buy your toy," said Aunt Dee Bee. "You must find a way to repair your toy and become the keeper of its beauty. Give your toy a reason to want to be yours." Looking at the girls she said, "that is my price."

"I don't understand," said Toy.

Aunt Dee Bee looked at the girls and said, "A long time ago I was a little girl and I loved those toys. I'm sad to say that I neglected them and didn't take care of them. They became old and ugly. I just threw them away. I feel bad about that now and I want you girls to return the love that I once took away from them. Can you do that?"

Toy shook her head up and down and Dew Drop searched the face of Aunt Dee Bee. "We will try very hard to give them as much love as we can."

"That is all I can ask," said Aunt Dee Bee.

Returning her eyes to Honey Bee, she said, "I haven't heard from you, Honey Bee."

Dew Drop was hoping Honey Bee would say the right thing. She didn't want her to blow it for them.

Honey Bee had dropped her head and in a small voice said, "I have some of my own toys that I didn't take care of."

"Well, I guess you girls have some things to think about. I will look forward to seeing you tomorrow."

Walking down a long lane, the girls were very quiet. No one said a word. They reached the fork in the road and said their good-byes.

"See you tomorrow, Honey Bee!"

"Okay! See yeah!"

Dew Drop and Toy walked slowly home. Their dog Laddie was glad to see them. He wagged his tail and licked Dew Drop's hand.

"Hi!" said the girls.

Rubbing his head, the girls hurried to get home.

"Come on, boy! I'll play with you later," said Dew Drop.

Everyone seemed to be busy working. Mr. Clagghorn was in the cherry tree picking cherries. Mr. Blew-it was mowing grass in the field, and mum was canning peaches. Claude de Ball was playing in his playpen as usual.

"Hi, Mum! Can we help you do something? We were at Aunt Dee Bee's with Honey Bee."

"Go wash your hands and you can tell all about your day."

The girls chattered away while they worked. "Do you know that Aunt Dee Bee has an attic full of toys and things? She said we could have a toy if we took care of it. What do you think, Mum?"

Sweet Pearl looked at the girls and smiled. "I

think you have enough junk to take care of. We don't need anymore."

The girls were dumb-struck! "What? This isn't junk. She has some real treasures," said Dew Drop.

Mum laughed. "Well, if you only bring one toy home, I guess it will be all right."

"That's one toy for each of us, Mum."

She looked at the faces of her girls and knew she couldn't say no.

"All right. One toy for each of you."

"Oh, thanks," said the girls.

While the girls worked beside their mother, they sang songs and laughed at the animals playing around them. Mum was glad they came home to help her. Time went faster and the girls always put a song in her heart.

Early the next morning, Honey Bee came to walk with the girls. Each girl was deep in thought. Dew Drop had decided she wanted the ballerina. She hoped Honey Bee didn't want it because she already had more toys than anyone she knew.

Toy had thoughts of her own. It was harder for her to choose. She really wanted the big rabbit with the chewed nose and missing ear. He needed her the most. She didn't care that the rabbit was as big as she was. He needed her to love him.

Toy was dreaming last night and she dreamed about the vase. There was something about the lady's face that drew her to the vase. The beautiful painted lady haunted her dreams. She knew her from somewhere, but couldn't remember where.

"What should I do?" Honey Bee drew Toy away from her thoughts.

"Have you girls decided what toy you want?"

Dew Drop knew better than to tell her. She might decide she wanted the toy they had chosen.

"No, Toy and I haven't decided yet."

"What did you decide, Honey Bee?"

"I think I would like the hobby horse. I don't have one and I think it would look real nice in my room."

"That's a good choice," Dew Drop was relieved.

157

The girls were in deep thought. What were they
to do? Reaching the old house, the girls couldn't
wait to make their choices. Aunt Dee Bee followed
them up the stairs. The steps were long and narrow
and they creaked with every step. Honey Bee pulled
the light chain and walked inside. She looked at the
hobby horse and all it needed was a little paint.

"This is my choice," said Honey Bee.

"Fine! It's yours."

Dew Drop was relieved. She picked up the round
pink jewelry box. The ballerina was small but she
was beautiful. Her eyes were black just like Dew
Drop's. "May I have this music box?"

"Of course! It's yours."

Aunt Dee Bee watched Toy as she looked at the
vase. Then she went over and hugged the ragged
rabbit standing by the window.

"I really wanted the vase, but the rabbit needs
me to love him," she said.

Looking at Aunt Dee Bee, Toy said in a small
voice, "The lady whose face is painted on the vase

looks like someone I know. Do you know who she is?"

Aunt Dee Bee didn't know what to say, so she lied and said, "No, honey. I don't know her."

"You know, Toy, I think maybe your mother would like to have the vase. I will give you the vase and the rabbit if you would like it."

Toy looked into her eyes and was surprised to see she was smiling. "Oh! Thank you! I will take real good care of them."

They spent the rest of the morning with Aunt Dee Bee and Honey Bee made arrangements for her father to pick up her rocking horse. They had a fun time, but now it was time to go home.

Watching the girls go down the lane with their toys, Aunt Dee Bee couldn't help but fall in love with Toy. She was special and someday she would make sure Toy belonged to her.

Chattering as fast as their mouths could go, the girls talked about their day with Aunt Dee Bee. Mum said she could help repair the rabbit and make

him as good as new. Toy knew all along that her
Mum could fix anything.

Later that night while they were getting ready for
bed, Dew Drop asked Toy why she didn't give
Mum the vase.

Looking at Dew Drop with big eyes Toy said,
"The vase is special and I know it. I want to give it
to her as a special gift. I will know when the time is
right."

Reaching under her bed she placed the vase in a
shoe box and hurried to hide it before mum came
into the room to pray with them.

"I hope you know what you are doing!" said
Dew Drop.

The hours in the day were never long enough for
the girls. Toy kept her secret hidden under the bed.
Mum helped Dew Drop and Toy sew a new face for
her rabbit. The mouth was made with heavy carpet
cord and, of course, he had a big smile stretching
clear across his face. His nose was made with heavy
brown felt material. The rabbit's huge eyes were

circled with black cord. The missing ear was replaced with a huge, pink, floppy ear falling down his smiling face. The ear covered one of his eyes and he looked like he was winking at the girls. The rabbit had taken on a whole new look.

"What are you going to name your rabbit?" asked Dew Drop.

"I'm not sure if it is a boy or girl," said Toy. "I'll have to decide later. There must be a special name for him, or her."

Dew Drop laughed and helped Toy place her rabbit in the corner of their room.

*

While the girls were having fun with the rabbit, Aunt Dee Bee was making plans to take Toy from her home. She wanted a sweet child of her own. Her mind was all confused and she was about to do something that would hurt a lot of people.

Never ever go with anyone alone! Your parents must always know who you are with at all times. It could save your life. Most of all (Obey all Rules.)

Dew Drop and Toy knew the rules. The only problem was they didn't always obey them.

One hot night the whole family was playing hide and seek. Mr. Clagghorn and Mr. Blew-it were very hard for the girls to find. Sometimes they just gave up looking. It was Toy's turn to hide her eyes.

BE CAREFUL TOY!!

CHAPTER 12

THE PRETTY FACE

"OLLIE, OLLIE—IN FREE!" cried the kids. Poor Toy had looked and looked for the kids. She couldn't find any of them.

"Where is she?" asked Mr. Blew-it.

Laughing, the children decided they would all have to find her.

"She always does this and we have to take our time and go and find her," said Mr. Clagghorn.

The children searched and searched for her.

"TOY! COME ON OUT!...Silence. We are tired of looking for you. We give up! You have the best hiding spot. This isn't funny anymore."

There wasn't even a sound. Mr. Blew-it was starting to get scared.

"You guys go home and get Daddy Waggs. Something isn't right here. Bring some lanterns and flashlights with you. I'll keep looking until you get back. Now hurry!"

Dew Drop and Mr. Clagghorn ran home as fast as they could. Their hearts were beating so fast they could hear it pounding in their ears. They were afraid that something terrible had happened to her.

Dew Drop was crying and great gulps of tears stuck in her throat. They reached the front porch and Daddy Waggs greeted them. He was sitting on the swing.

"Why are you two in such a hurry?"

There was a full moon and he could see the terrible look of pain on their faces.

"What's wrong?" he asked.

Dew Drop ran to her father's arms, and Mr. Clagghorn started to stutter.

"We---we were playing hide and seek and it was Toy's turn to find us. He blurted out that she had disappeared and was no where to be seen. We looked everywhere and still we couldn't find her."

"WHAT? Grab some lanterns and we will go and look for her. Dew Drop stay here! I don't want you to get lost too."

Dew Drop watched Daddy Waggs and Mr. Clagghorn run in the direction of the barn. Crying she ran in the house and sobbed her story to her Mum. Sweet Pearl was worried but tried not to show it.

Taking Dew Drop in her arms she said, "Don't worry honey. I'm sure she was just playing a game. They will find her. Just you wait and see."

Daddy Waggs and the boys looked for hours. Yelling her name over and over again, all they heard was silence. The animals didn't even make any sounds. Shaking his head, Daddy Waggs was sure this was some kind of sick joke.
"Come on Sweetheart! Come out and we will forget all about this foolishness. Please come out!"

His voice was fading in the silence. He felt afraid and defeated. Laddie their dog was sniffing around but came up with nothing.

"Come on, boys. I think we need to go and see the sheriff."

Deep in the pit of his stomach was a hole; a big empty hole. Mr. Blew-it looked at his father and saw a look of deep pain on his face. He didn't say anything because he didn't have the words to say. Mr. Clagghorn wiped the tears that were rolling down his face.

"Please God, keep her safe."

Mum was rocking Claude de Ball when they finally came home. She laid him in his bed and closed the door. Wringing her hands, she looked at John and said, "Where is she?"

*

"I don't want to stay here. My Mum and Daddy will be worried about me."

Tears rolling down her cheeks, Toy was begging Aunt Dee Bee to let her go home.

"Now, now, Toy! Don't make a big fuss out of nothing. You can stay here tonight and if you're good, I might let you go home tomorrow. I am really disappointed in you. You know I would never hurt you."

Closing the door behind her, Aunt Dee Bee took one last look at the little girl she wanted as her own. "Good-night—and when I see you tomorrow, I want to see you smiling."

A metal sound scraped the door. Toy knew she was locked in. *Why was this happening to her?*

Silent tears rolled down her cheeks. Toy was so angry with herself for coming along with Aunt Dee Bee. She saw her hiding behind the barn and Toy thought it was Mr. Blew-it. Toy shivered as she thought of the way she was tricked into believing Aunt Dee Bee was going to help her find the kids.

Aunt Dee Bee had a strange look in her eyes. Her eyes had a deep, dark look. Toy tried to think of the words to describe her eyes. Blank and empty were the words. She looked straight at Toy, but she didn't seem to see her. Toy had never seen anyone with eyes with no expression or warmth.

Frightened and sick to her stomach, Toy laid her head down on her pillow. She closed her eyes and prayed that God would help her to get back home.

Dew Drop couldn't sleep either. She tried to think where Toy might be. Tomorrow she was going to find Mr. Warts and see if he might help her find Toy. Maybe the animals may have seen where she went.

Dew Drop fell to her knees and the words poured from her heart. "Oh, please God keep her safe. *Watch over her and protect her from the Evil One.*"

The blue jay circled the sky and screamed his alarm to the rest of the valley animals. They came out of their homes one by one to see what was going on. There didn't seem to be much danger. They stood on their hind legs and sniffed the air.

Hairy O'Dor, the skunk, asked Grey Heel the rabbit what was going on.

Flye-Bye, the squirrel, spoke up and said, "Someone is missing. Who—who! I don't know who!"

"You sound like that scruffy old owl," said Hairy O'Dor the skunk.

"EXCU-U-S-S-E ME!"

168

One by one the animals came into the middle of the valley. They stood at attention to see if the preacher boy was going to tell them another story.

Mr. Clagghorn had called them all together to ask them if anyone had seen Toy the night she disappeared. Dew Drop and Mr. Warts came with him.

The animals felt so sorry for them. The little girl cried and the preacher boy wiped his eyes.

"We are so worried," he said. "Please! Can you tell us anything?"

The animals shook their heads and one by one came up to Dew Drop and rubbed their furry bodies on her legs. Through her tears she knew that the animals cared about her and Toy.

Walking back to the house, all three were feeling very sad.

Looking at Mr. Warts Dew Drop said, "I don't understand what happened to her. She couldn't have just disappeared, could she?" Never in her wildest dreams did she think that someone took her.

Mr. Warts hugged her and told her that somehow he knew Toy was all right.

Mr. Warts walked back to his cottage and promised Dew Drop that he would pray for Toy. He couldn't believe that he made such a promise. It has been years since he prayed.

The people in the village of Nannyglow had taken turns looking for Toy. She had just disappeared. All the neighbors searched and searched for her. Aunt Dee Bee had made them coffee and pound cake while they searched.

The long days turned into a long week. The sheriff talked to every stranger in town. The animals kept vigils taking turns looking for the sweet little girl. Where could she be?

Mum tried to keep busy cleaning the house. She decided to clean the girls' room. She picked up clothes and changed the bed. Mum stubbed her toe on something hard under the bed.

What could that be, she thought. She got down on her hands and knees and searched for the object under the bed. She found an old shoe box.

"What in the world is this," she said to herself. Opening the box, she couldn't believe her eyes. She hadn't seen this vase since she was a young girl.

Yelling for Dew Drop, Mum fell on the bed. Running up the stairs, Dew Drop was frightened that something had happened.

"Mum, what's wrong?"

Tears running down Mum's face, she asked Dew Drop, "Where did this come from and how did you get it?"

Dew Drop just stared at the vase.

"TELL ME! NOW!"

Dew Drop was afraid of the tone of her voice.

"What does it matter? It's just an old vase that Aunt Dee Bee gave to Toy to give to you. She said that you would like it. Toy wanted to wait and give it to you as a special gift."

"Dew Drop, go get your father! I think I know where Toy is. Hurry!"

Dew Drop ran as fast as she could to get her father. She was running as if the devil himself were chasing her.

*

"Sing, little Toy girl, sing!"

Toy was sitting on the piano bench while Aunt Dee Bee played. Toy tried to croak out the words to My Bonnie lies over the ocean. My Bonnie lies over the sea. My Bonnie lies over the ocean; so bring back My Bonnie to me.

"I can't sing anymore," cried Toy.

"Sing or I'll put you back in your room."

Tears rolled down Toy's cheeks. She had sat at that piano all morning singing the same old song.

Toy was about to give up and go to her room when they heard loud pounding at the door. Aunt Dee Bee just sat at the piano. Toy ran towards the door and tried to open it. The door was too heavy for her to open.

Yelling as loud as she could Toy said, "I can't get it open!"

She heard her daddy's voice telling her to get back and they would kick it in. THUMP! The door came crashing down. Standing on the porch was her daddy, mum, Mr. Blew-it, the sheriff, and Honey Bee's father. Toy ran into her father's waiting arms, and hugged and kissed him through her tears.

"Are you all right?"

"Oh! Daddy, I was so scared. Aunt Dee Bee isn't the same old lady that I always liked. She looks at me with funny eyes. She needs someone to help her."

Mum kissed Toy and walked to the piano. Aunt Dee Bee had her hands over her eyes crying. Mum sat beside her and put her arms around her and she did the oddest thing. Mum cried with her.

"Thank you for taking care of my baby. I know you didn't mean to take her from us."

Aunt Dee Bee moved away from the piano and looked everyone in the eye.

"I'm sorry about all this fuss. I don't even have anything for you to eat."

Staring at her brother through tearful eyes, she said, "I was just trying to bring Bonnie back to us. I didn't mean to hurt anyone. Toy reminds me of her.

Aunt Dee Bee's brother put his arm around her and said, "We all know you didn't mean to hurt anyone, but you did. I think you had better come home with me so Candy and I can take care of you."

The sheriff helped Aunt Dee Bee into the car and told them he would file his report and would talk to everyone later. He asked Daddy Waggs if he was going to file charges.

Toy looked at her daddy and said, "How much are you charging her for taking care of me? You know I had to do everything myself. I fixed my own breakfast, helped with dishes and I even had to make my own bed. I think she owes us a lot of money for all the work I had to do."

Looking at Toy, they couldn't help but laugh at her innocent little face.

The church bells rang out in the village of Nannyglow. Everyone was rejoicing over the safe return of the little girl. Hugs and kisses from her brothers made Toy so thankful that she was home. She knew that home was a place that she would always be safe.

Dew Drop hugged Toy and gave her a lecture about going home with someone without telling her first.

"I thought I told you to stay close to me! You always get in trouble when you don't listen to me!"

Toy gave her a hug and said, "I missed you."

They both knew that Toy got in trouble when she listened to Dew Drop, but neither one of them said anything about that!

Later that night, mum gathered the children together and tried to explain why Aunt Dee Bee was not herself. "I think I need to tell you the story about myself and Aunt Dee Bee."

"One summer when we were teenagers, Dee and her sister Bonnie asked me to go on a vacation with them and their parents. We went to the beach and we were having the best time of our lives. They had

an art show and open air theaters. We went to a
great drama presentation and after the show; we met
a young artist who was very interested in Bonnie.

Bonnie was a beautiful girl with bright blue eyes
and long blonde hair. The artist painted her picture
on the vase that Aunt Dee Bee gave to Toy. They
spent every minute they could together.

Well, to make a long story short, Bonnie ran off
with the young man and never came back home
again. Sometime later, we heard that she became ill
and died. Dee never got over her sister leaving and
running away. Toy looks like Bonnie a little bit.
Aunt Dee Bee thought for a short time that if Toy
stayed with her she could, in her mind, bring
Bonnie back to her."

"Do you think that Aunt Dee Bee wants the vase
back?" asked Toy.

Mum looked at Toy and was so thankful to God
that Toy was back home with them.

"Why don't we visit her in a few days and ask
her ourselves?"

The children were all very quiet and they all felt sorry for Aunt Dee Bee. Mr. Clagghorn spoke and said, "What's going to happen to her?"

Mum said she was under a doctor's care and would be staying with her brother and his family.

"Now I think it's time for bed. Don't forget to pray."

Dew Drop and Toy were getting ready for bed. They sat down and looked in each other's eyes.

"Promise me you will never run away with some silly boy," cried Dew Drop.

Toy hugged her sister and they both made a promise to stay best friends for always and always.

"We will never get married unless we can always live close to each other. We want our children to be best friends."

Wiping away their tears, they crawled into their beds. They were glad to be home sleeping beside each other.

Toy kept many secrets in her heart. She knew that Bonnie was the angel that protected her. She knew that the pretty face on the vase was her very own angel. The room was dark, but Toy could see a filmy white haze swirling around her bed. A hushed voice filtered in the air. *Hushed and sweet was the voice who told her to keep their secret forever.*

Toy whispered, *"Forever."*

#

Later that night a shadow appeared in their room. Dew Drop opened her eyes the best she could but couldn't tell who it was. Her mind must be playing tricks on her. She squinted her eyes and thought it must be the candy-colored sandman. He sprinkled star dust and whispered, *"Go to sleep. Everything will be all right."*

Closing her eyes, she drifted off to sleep once again. The sandman looks like Daddy Waggs, she thought. Oh No! That couldn't be; *or could it?*

John closed the door and leaned against its frame. He always looked in on his children before he went to bed. The love he felt for his children was wrapped tightly around his heart. He had little money, but he had wealth that couldn't be measured by the size of his wallet. John and Evelyn were wealthy, indeed!

*

Good night to all our new friends and may God bless.

PROVERBS 20:11

Even a child is known by his actions, whether his conduct is pure and right.

(NIV)

ISBN 141200023-8